STAR QUALITY

STAR QUALITY

Jean Ure

HarperCollins *Children's Books*

First published in Great Britain by
HarperCollins *Children's Books* in 2017
HarperCollins *Children's Books* is a division of HarperCollins*Publishers* Ltd,
HarperCollins Publishers
1 London Bridge Street
London SE1 9GF

The HarperCollins website address is:
www.harpercollins.co.uk
1

ISBN 978-0-00-816453-9

Jean Ure asserts the moral right to be identified as the author of the work.

Typeset in Gill Sans 12/20pt by Palimpsest Book Production Ltd,
Falkirk, Stirlingshire

Printed and bound by
CPI Group (UK) Ltd, Croydon, CR0 4YY

MIX
Paper from
responsible sources
FSC™ C007454

Chapter One

"Honestly," squealed Caitlyn, "I nearly died!"

"I know, I know!" That was Roz, also screaming. "I just wanted to bury myself under the floorboards!"

"Me, too!" Alex rolled her eyes, rather wildly. "I thought I was going to pass out on the spot!"

"That moment when she walked in…"

"Omigod!"

Now they were all squealing. A woman walking past gave us a very odd look. I wasn't surprised! They sounded like a load of fingernails scraping down a blackboard. All high-pitched and shrill. Quite painful, really. And all because – shock, horror! – Madam had suddenly appeared in the middle of class!

★ 1 ☆

I gave a little squeak, just to show that I was sympathetic. I didn't want to seem stand-offish; they were, after all, my friends. Caitlyn was actually my *best* friend. We'd spent most of the day together, taking our final audition for the City Ballet School – including the class that Madam had walked in on.

I expect most people would have thought it was a bit stressful. Even the class itself, with or without Madam's laser-like presence. Just knowing all the time that you were being assessed, like "Is she musical enough? Is she supple enough? Has she got what it takes?" Though to be honest, it wasn't so very different from what we were used to. The four of us had been taking special classes at the school every Saturday morning for the past year. Extension classes they called them, for people who were hoping to join the school as full-time students. We'd already got through the preliminary auditions so we'd known what to expect. Class the same as usual; just a bit more demanding. More stretches and jumps, more complicated series of steps. It was what we'd been working towards. Miss Jackson, who'd taken us on Saturday mornings, had prepared us well. Once we'd started and I'd got over any jitters I might have had, I'd actually enjoyed myself. I think it was because it was a challenge. I do like to be challenged! I sometimes get bored otherwise and find it difficult to concentrate.

Following on from class we'd had a series of intelligence tests. I don't think any of us had been specially bothered about those. After all, it's not like they expect you to be a genius or anything. Just so long as you have *some* kind of a brain. And imagination. It's good to have imagination. Better really, if you ask me, than being able to do square roots and equations and stuff. (I probably just say that because I personally can't do them. But I have got imagination!)

After the intelligence tests we'd all had to have a medical exam, to check our bones were OK. Nothing really to worry about cos surely by now if there was anything wrong they'd have found out? Well, you'd think so, considering they'd already been teaching us for a year, though it's true that sometimes odd things can be discovered and people are told they're not physically right for a dancing career. Still, I'm what Dad calls "an incurable optimist". I don't believe in torturing myself by imagining all the things that could go wrong. Even the dreaded interview at the end with Miss Hickman, the Head of Dance Studies, hadn't really held any fears. I'd felt sure I'd think of something to say. I usually do!

It was true, on the other hand, that I had a bit of an unfair advantage. When you come from a ballet family – when your mum and dad, your brother, your sister, are all dancers – you tend to kind of take things for granted. Ballet just becomes an accepted part of your life, no more peculiar than – well! Eating and drinking. Going to bed. Getting up. It's just something you do.

It wasn't like that for the others, especially not for Caitlyn. It had been a real struggle for her. Alex and Roz hadn't come from ballet families, either, so I probably should try to be more understanding. Madam *was* quite a frightening sort of person and none of us had expected her to suddenly come teetering in, on her high heels, in the middle of class. She was the Director after all! Dame Catherine Le Brocq, MBE. (For Services to Dance.) She had been one of the founders of City Ballet. Generations of dancers had lived their lives in terror of her, going right back to when Mum was there. It was hard to picture Mum ever being terrified of anyone, but she had once confessed to me that "Madam used to turn us all to jelly." Even I had felt a slight twinge when the door had swung open and I'd seen her standing there, tiny as a sparrow with these diamond-sharp eyes shooting laser beams in all directions. I don't *think* I faltered cos Mum had trained me well, but it was a bit of a shock. I couldn't really blame the others for being petrified.

"I thought it was just going to be an ordinary class!" wailed Caitlyn.

"I *know*!" squealed Roz. "So did I!"

"Actually," I said, "it *was* just an ordinary class."

They all turned, reproachfully, to look at me.

"How can you *say* that?" cried Alex.

"I mean, apart from Madam it was ordinary. If she hadn't suddenly appeared—"

"But she did suddenly appear!"

"Yes, but she didn't stay for very long."

"Long enough," moaned Roz.

"I just got totally *lost*." Caitlyn's eyes had gone all big at the memory of it. "If I hadn't been able to follow Maddy, I'd never have got through it! I knew *she'd* get it right cos she always does."

She said it without any show of envy. Like it was just a simple fact: *Maddy always gets things right*. Maybe I did, but that was only cos I'd been at it so long. Right from when I was about three years old. It would be a bit shameful if I *didn't* get things right.

"Weren't you scared at *all*?" said Alex.

I said, "Well, I was, but only just for a minute and then I kind of forgot about her."

"All right for some," grumbled Roz. "You probably spent half your time as a baby sitting on her lap."

★ 6 ☆

I giggled. The thought of me, or anyone else, sitting on Madam's lap was quite funny. Sean – who's my brother and a lead dancer with the Company – once said that Madam was more likely to bite a baby's head off than cuddle it: "She is a scary, scary woman."

And Sean is one of her favourites! She rules the Company with a rod of iron, but Sean has always known how to get round her.

We all turned down The Cut towards Waterloo Station to catch our different trains home. Some people had come to the audition accompanied by their mums, but they were mostly the ones who'd had long journeys to make. The four of us were local and used to travelling in on Tubes and trains. Caitlyn and I actually lived quite near each other and even went to the same school.

"As a matter of interest," said Alex, "what did you say in your interview? When they asked you, '*Why do you want to dance?*'"

"I just told them the truth," said Caitlyn. "I said cos it's what I've always dreamt of doing."

"Even though you didn't start till so late?"

Unlike the rest of us, who'd mostly had our first ballet lessons at five or six, Caitlyn hadn't been able to start until she was eleven. It wasn't because she hadn't wanted to. She'd been desperate!

"Not everybody," I reminded Alex, "can afford to pay for dancing lessons." Specially not a single mum struggling to make ends meet, like Caitlyn's mum.

"Oh. Right! I was forgetting." Alex nodded, sympathetically. "They'll have given you a plus for that."

"Do you really think so?" Caitlyn looked at her, anxiously. "I thought they might hold it against me."

"No, they'll say it shows single-mindedness and determination and means you really know what you want."

"So what did *you* say?" said Roz.

"Me?" Alex pulled a face. "I just said I loved to dance. I couldn't think of anything clever! What about you?"

"Don't ask!" Roz gave another squeal. "It was awful – I just burbled on completely mindlessly… all about how I'd been taken to see *Swan Lake* as a child and how I'd fallen in love with it and wanted to be able to spin round and round like Odile and her thirty-two *fouettés*!"

"You mean you actually counted them?"

"No, it was the person sitting behind me… I didn't even know that's what they were! I went straight back home and tried to do some in my bedroom."

Alex said, "*Wow.* How many did you manage?"

"I didn't manage any! I bashed into the wardrobe and nearly knocked my knee cap off. I'm so ashamed," moaned Roz. "Why did I have to go and tell them something so stupid?"

"It's not stupid," said Caitlyn. "I expect they quite enjoyed hearing about it."

"A lot more fun than just saying you loved to dance," agreed Alex. She tapped her forehead. "Shows imagination."

"What about Maddy?" They all turned, in my direction. "What did you say?"

"Oh." I shrugged. "I just said I couldn't imagine doing

anything else. So Miss Hickman asked me if I'd ever actually tried imagining, and I said no, I wouldn't dare."

They gaped at me. "You wouldn't *dare?*" said Roz.

"Cos of Mum and what she'd have to say. It was a joke; it was a joke!"

"You are so brave," said Caitlyn.

I hadn't felt particularly brave. The words had just come tumbling out of me, as words do.

"Did anyone laugh?" said Alex.

"Um… well… not exactly *laugh*. Miss Hickman sort of twitched her lips."

"Like she found it funny?"

"Well… I suppose."

I felt suddenly doubtful. Miss Hickman is Head of Dance Studies. According to Sean, she is not noted for her sense of humour. Maybe she *hadn't* found it funny? Maybe I shouldn't have said it? Mum is always accusing me of not thinking before I speak.

"Oh, well," said Roz. "At least it's over. Now we just have to wait."

We all promised to keep in touch and let one another know the minute we heard anything, then Alex and Roz peeled off to catch their trains while me and Caitlyn headed for the Underground.

"How long do you think it'll be?" said Caitlyn.

"Before we hear? About a week, according to Mum."

"I wish they'd tell us on the spot! A week's like for *ever*. Why does it take them so long?"

"I suppose they have to go and… I don't know!" I waved a hand. "Discuss things."

"What sort of things?" Caitlyn's face had gone all puckered. "What would they need to discuss?"

"Well, like, maybe if there was someone they weren't quite sure of? Or if they can only take, say, ten people and have to decide which ones they're going to turn down?" As soon as I'd said it, I wished I hadn't. Now I'd gone and terrified her. "There isn't any point worrying," I said. "We've done our best."

I nearly added that in any case I felt sure they wouldn't turn down any of Mum's students. Mum was one of

★ 11 ☆

their own! Plus she has this reputation as one of the very best teachers in the country and only ever enters students she has complete faith in. But suppose just for once they actually did turn someone down? After I'd practically given Caitlyn my word that she could be certain of a place?

"Let's face it," I said, "we wouldn't have been accepted for special classes if they didn't think we were promising."

"But you just said... we can't all get in! *You* will, cos—"

"Cos what?" I said. "Cos of who my family is?"

"No! Cos you're a good dancer and you've been doing it for ever."

"You're a good dancer," I said. "Mum wouldn't have given you a scholarship if she didn't think you had what it takes."

"But I still haven't properly caught up!" She meant because of starting so late. "You're all so far ahead of me!"

It was true that Caitlyn didn't have the strongest technique, which perhaps was a bit of a worry. But they always said it wasn't necessarily technique they were looking for so much as what Mum calls potential, like having the right sort of body and being able to move naturally to the music.

"If I don't get in —" Caitlyn gave a deep, quivering sigh — "I shall feel like I've let your mum down. *And* you."

I might have added, "And Sean," but it would only have embarrassed her. Like lots of other ballet fans she had this massive crush on him. Even now she couldn't say his name without blushing. But he was the one, in the end, who had persuaded Mum to give Caitlyn a chance. I'd been nagging at her for ages without getting anywhere. It wasn't till Sean had seen what Caitlyn could do that he had stepped in and worked his magic.

"Don't worry," I said. "You'll get in; I'm sure you will!"

Oh, I did hope so! It would be too terrible if she

didn't make it. After all those long years when becoming a dancer – even just having ballet lessons – had been nothing but a dream. If anyone deserved a chance, it was Caitlyn.

When I got home I found that Jen was there. She'd brought James round to show him off to Mum. James is my nephew. Imagine me, an auntie! I am not much into babies as a rule, but James is really quite sweet. Even Mum adores him, though she'd been so cross when Jen had announced she was going to give up her career to stay at home and be a mum. It wasn't what you were supposed to do! It certainly wasn't what Mum had done. It was only after having me that she'd finally given up performing, but she'd been in her forties by then so she'd probably have had to retire anyway. She wasn't the sort to be happy playing old lady parts. Fairy godmothers and the like. I won't be, either! I'll probably become a teacher, like Mum. I had, after all, been Caitlyn's teacher for the first few months, until Sean had become involved and helped change her daydream into reality. Even Mum, who is so horribly critical, had been forced to admit I'd done a good job. If Caitlyn was offered a place at CBS, I could pat myself on the back cos it would be partly thanks to me! *But please, please, please,* I thought, *let her be accepted!*

Jen and Mum were both eager to hear how the audition had gone. I said that it had gone OK, in spite of Madam suddenly bursting in on us.

"Ooh, scary!" said Jen.

"I know," I said. "It terrified the life out of some people."

"Not you, I'll bet!"

I said, "No, I hardly noticed." And then, in case maybe that sounded a bit like boasting: "Maybe just at first… when she first came in."

I went up on my toes, being Madam in her high heels, surveying the room with narrowed eyes.

"Very amusing," said Mum. "Just remember, however, that this is the woman who holds your fate in her hands."

"All I'm saying –" I sank back down – "is I didn't *let*

myself be scared. Cos I thought what you would say...
CONCENTRATE!"

"Quite right," said Mum. "I'm glad my words seem to have sunk in."

Jen shook her head. "Always so confident! I remember my audition... I was a nervous wreck for days before. *And* afterwards, waiting to hear. Waiting to hear was almost the worst part. I don't think I had a single fingernail left by the time we got the letter!"

"What about Sean?" I said. I must have been about four years old when he'd had his audition. Too young to really remember very much. "Was he a nervous wreck?"

"You have to be joking!" said Jen. "When have you ever known Sean be a nervous wreck about anything? I've always envied you two... You sail through life, the pair of you, full steam ahead, not a worry in the world."

"Yes, sometimes a bit too sure of themselves," agreed Mum. "A touch of humility now and again might not come amiss."

She nodded rather pointedly in my direction. I felt quite indignant. Why pick on me? I wasn't the one people went all gooey over. *I* wasn't one of Madam's favourites!

"I have loads of humility," I said.

"You think?" said Jen. She laughed, and so did Mum.

"You and Sean both!" said Mum.

They were being totally unfair. Mum is the first to say you have to have faith in your abilities. I know what my good points are, but I know what my bad ones are, too. I would be the first to admit I am not as lyrical as, for instance, Caitlyn. I don't think Sean is that lyrical, either. I once saw him in *Sylphides*, all dreamy and romantic in the moonlight. Definitely not him! Perhaps me and Sean *were* a bit alike. I savoured the thought, testing it to see how I felt. I decided that I liked it! When I was little, Sean was one of my heroes, especially when he got into the Company, and then, later on, when he was promoted to soloist and everyone had heard of him. I enjoyed having a brother that all my friends had secret crushes on. Well, or not so secret, in Caitlyn's case! I wondered if anyone would ever have a crush on me when I got into the Company. *If* I got into the Company. If, if, *if*, touch wood!

It was just that I couldn't imagine *not* getting in. Mum, Dad, Jen – they had all been with City Ballet. Sean was one of their stars. How could I not follow in their footsteps? The Company was almost like a second family!

But Caitlyn was almost like family, too. We both had to get in! *Not just me. Please, please, please,* I thought once more. *Please let Caitlyn be accepted!*

I am never quite sure that I believe in God, but on the other hand I don't think it hurts to say the occasional prayer. Just in case there is someone there and they happen to be listening. So long as it's not for something silly, or selfish. Like one time when I prayed I would get through a maths test OK, even though I hadn't bothered to do any revision. I came next to bottom, but I didn't hold it against God as I don't believe that is what prayer is really supposed to be for. It is supposed (in my opinion) to be for other people. In this case, for Caitlyn.

Mentally I closed my eyes and put my hands together. *God*, I thought, *if you're listening, please do the right thing!*

Chapter Two

It was over a week, now, and we still hadn't heard. Every morning as I arrived at school, Caitlyn would greet me with a heart-rending wail: "It hasn't come yet! Has yours?" She meant, of course, the letter. The one we were all waiting for.

"Surely," I said to Mum, "we should have heard by now?"

"You'll hear," said Mum. "Don't worry."

"I'm not worried for me," I said. And then, very quickly, before I could be accused of being over-confident, I said, "Well, I suppose perhaps I am just a *little* bit. Cos that's only natural, isn't it? Being a *little* bit worried. Anyone would be! Even Sean. I mean—"

"Maddy, stop babbling," said Mum. "What's the problem?"

"It's Caitlyn," I said. "I'm worried for Caitlyn! Mum, she will be OK, won't she? She will get in?"

"I'd certainly like to think so," said Mum. "I wouldn't have let her take the audition if I didn't believe she stood a fair chance. But even if she doesn't make it this time round, it's not the end of the world. She can always try again next year, when she's a bit more sure of herself."

I stared at Mum, in disbelief. "You don't think she's going to make it?"

"I didn't say that! She may very well do so. But she desperately needs to build up her confidence. How did she take it when Madam walked in? Did it throw her?"

"It threw everybody," I said. "Even me, a little bit."

It hadn't really thrown me, but I didn't feel it was my place to go telling tales. If Caitlyn had wanted Mum to know she'd got in a hopeless muddle and lost her way, she'd have told her herself. All she'd said, when we'd arrived for our Friday-evening class with Mum, and Mum had asked her how things had gone, was, "All right. I think." And then, a bit cheekily, she'd added, "Nowhere near as frightening as when I took my audition with you!"

I'd thought that was quite brave of her. Making a joke with Mum! Far braver than me making a joke with Miss Hickman. I also thought that it might actually have been true, since in some ways Mum is even more scary than Madam. But would Caitlyn still manage to be brave if she didn't get in along with the rest of us? If me, and Alex, and Roz, all made it and she didn't?

Mum must have guessed what I was thinking.

"Even if Caitlyn doesn't have your confidence," she said, "she's not going to give up that easily. She's had to fight for far too long and far too hard to fall at the first hurdle."

"But, Mum," I cried, "she'd be so upset!"

"She would," agreed Mum. "Certainly to begin with.

But if you want to get anywhere in life you have to be prepared to pick yourself up and carry on. I think you'll find Caitlyn has more backbone than you imagine."

All the same, I thought, it would be miserable going off to ballet school on my own. Perhaps my prayers *were* just a little bit for me as well as for Caitlyn, because how would I be able to enjoy myself, knowing how she would be feeling? And how would I ever be able to break it to her that I had got in when she hadn't?

"It's good that you're loyal," said Mum, "but give Caitlyn some credit... In spite of that meek exterior, she's no pushover!"

I knew Mum was right. Caitlyn had been struggling to teach herself ballet for a whole year before I'd discovered what she was up to and had started to help her. Every day without fail she had practised in her bedroom, and later on in the gym before school, when no one else was around, copying steps out of some of the many ballet books she had.

It was hard enough doing class every day when you had a dragon like Mum breathing down your neck. Mum wouldn't accept any excuses! Well, other than injury. Not even I would ever have dared to say I didn't feel like it. Not even when I'd had a streaming cold or loads of homework or just a general feeling of fed-upness. I honestly wasn't sure I'd have had the discipline to carry on all by myself, as Caitlyn had done. Obviously Caitlyn had never had any feelings of fed-upness. Never once had she lost sight of her dream.

Dreams can seem such flimsy things! I always picture them as being like puffy white clouds, high up in the sky, floating along quite happily until – *poof!* – a sudden gust of wind comes by and blows them to pieces, and all we're left with is little bits and pieces, scattered through the universe.

Caitlyn's dreams had obviously been made of sterner stuff. No gust of wind had ever come bursting into her daydreams. She had this fierce determination which had driven her on. But even the fiercest determination needed some encouragement!

Mum shook her head. "Maddy, you can't fight other people's battles for them," she said. "You did all you could. Now it's up to Caitlyn."

I sighed. Common sense was all very well, but I did so want us to be together!

The next day, when I turned in at the school gates, I found Caitlyn waiting for me. Her face was one big beam.

"It came!" she cried.

"The letter?"

"Yes!"

"You got in?"

I didn't really need to ask. The beam told me everything.

"I still can't believe it! I honestly never thought I would. Not after messing up like that. I thought they'd just tell me to go away and not bother them. It's all thanks to you! If I hadn't been able to watch what you were doing, I—" She broke off. "You did get yours?" She looked at me, anxiously. "You did hear?"

"Not yet," I said.

"Oh." Her face fell. "Maybe it'll be waiting for you when you get home."

"Maybe," I said. "Don't worry about it. The main thing is that you've got in!"

"I won't tell anyone," promised Caitlyn. "Not till you've heard, as well!"

I struggled for a bit, then said, "That's OK. You can tell people."

I knew she must be dying to. But Caitlyn said no, it wouldn't be fair. "We'll wait till we can both do it."

"What about Mum?" I said. "You ought to tell Mum! And Sean. You've *got* to tell Sean. Give him a call right now!"

"Now?" She looked shocked. "He might be asleep."

"So wake him up! It's good news; he'll be happy. Go on, quick, before we have to go into class."

"Wouldn't it be better if you did it?" she said.

I said, "Me? Why me? I'm not the one that's got good news!"

"*Please*, Maddy." She clasped her hands together. "You do it! Then you can tell your mum, as well."

I shook my head. "You are such a coward," I said.

He was my brother, for goodness' sake! And in spite of being one of Madam's favourites and one of the Company's leading dancers, he is one of the easiest people to talk to. Unlike some I could name (but won't cos it could be libel), he doesn't have any sort of star complex. Caitlyn really ought to know him well enough by now. It was high time she got over her schoolgirl crush! But it didn't seem fair to nag her, specially when she'd been so noble and self-sacrificing about keeping her audition result a secret until I'd had mine.

I did rather wonder why my letter hadn't yet come. I knew it wouldn't be waiting for me when I got in cos the post had already arrived when I'd left that morning.

"D'you think the others have heard?" I said.

The minute I said it, Caitlyn turned pink all over again.

I said, "They *have*?"

"They texted me this morning," she said. "They've both got in."

"Why didn't they text *me*?"

"Cos they knew I'd tell you?"

"But they're my friends as much as yours! Why didn't they text both of us?"

"Maybe because... cos we all *know* you'll get in. You're, like... up there –" she raised a hand above her head – "and we're, like, sort of..."

"Sort of what?"

"What I mean –" she was starting to sound a bit desperate – "it's like you're royalty!"

I said, "*What*?"

"Your mum and dad! You're like a sort of royal family. Of the ballet world," she added, hastily.

I stared at her, horrified. "That's completely mad! I'm just the same as the rest of you."

"You're not," said Caitlyn. "You know you're not. I'm very *glad* you're not, cos if it hadn't been for your mum..."

Who did sometimes behave a bit like royalty, I had to admit.

"We don't hold it against you," said Caitlyn, earnestly. "It's not like you boast about it or anything. It's just one of those things. You don't have to worry like the rest of us. But p'raps you shouldn't tell your mum about me getting in until you've heard, cos I'm sure you will tomorrow."

But although I hung around the following morning, waiting till the last possible moment, not a single letter came fluttering through the letter box. Caitlyn was in a state of jitters at the school gates, anxious in case the bell should ring before I got there.

"Did it come?" she cried.

I shook my head. "Not yet."

"Oh." Her face fell. "I was sure you'd have heard by now!"

"It's OK," I said. "As soon as I get home, I'm going to give Mum the good news about you."

Caitlyn opened her mouth to protest.

"No," I said, "I am! It's not fair to keep her waiting. She'll be so pleased when I tell her."

"But what about you?" wailed Caitlyn. "Why haven't you heard?"

I shrugged. "I dunno. Post, maybe? Letters are always getting lost." That, at any rate, was what Dad said. He had this theory that all over London there were huge bags of mail that posties had just dumped. "They've probably gone and put it through the wrong door, or something. I'm not bothered! It'll come."

I said I wasn't bothered, and it was true, I wasn't. Not really. I couldn't help thinking it was a bit odd, though. Caitlyn obviously thought so, too. I could tell that it was preying on her mind. At breaktime she rushed up to me and hissed, "I know why you haven't heard!"

I said, "Why?"

"Cos you're in the second half of the alphabet and we're all in the first!"

I frowned.

"It's got to be," said Caitlyn. "Think about it!"

"Mm… maybe." I supposed it made sense. Roz Costello, Alex Ellman, Caitlyn Hughes, Madeleine O'Brien. "I'm still going to tell Mum, though!"

I told her when I got back from school that afternoon, even though my letter still hadn't come. Dad was there as well. He said, "Caitlyn? This is your protégée that you've been nursing?"

"I knew it would pay off," said Mum. "I knew she had it in her!"

"It was me that discovered her," I said. "Me and Sean. What's a protégée?"

Dad groaned. "Don't they teach you anything at that school? *Protéger… to protect?*"

"You mean, like, Mum's been protecting her?"

"Guiding her," said Mum. "Mentoring, if you like."

Teaching, in other words. I opened my mouth to point

out – in case she had forgotten – that I was the one who'd taught her first, but Mum cut in ahead of me. "What I want to know is why Caitlyn's heard and you haven't?"

"Oh, we think that's just cos of me being in the second half of the alphabet," I said. "All the others are near the beginning."

"What others?" said Mum, rather sharply.

"Other people that have heard."

Mum's eyes narrowed.

"*Costello, Ellman, Hughes…*" I ticked them off on my fingers.

"They've all got in?"

Mum's gaze flickered across the room to where Dad was sitting.

Dad, very faintly, hunched a shoulder. "Probably just some administrative glitch."

"Not good enough!" snapped Mum. "Totally unacceptable! If she hasn't heard by tomorrow, I'm going to be on that telephone demanding to speak to someone."

"Oh, Mum, no, don't, please!" I begged. It was bad enough everyone thinking I was like some kind of royalty, just because of who my parents were. I had been quite shocked that Roz and Alex had chosen to tell Caitlyn their good news and not me, simply cos of thinking I was above it all. I wasn't above it all! I didn't expect special treatment. I never *got* special treatment. If anything, Mum was harder on me than on anyone else when she took us for class. She was positively soft on Caitlyn! She never chewed *her* out or accused her of having arms like waterlogged balloons, like she'd once done to me. But she does undeniably have a lot of influence, and friends in high places, and I desperately didn't want her wading in on my behalf. I could just hear her. "*This is Madeleine O'Brien's mother. I'm wondering why it is that my daughter hasn't yet had her letter of acceptance... I presume it is on its way?*"

My toes were curling in shame just at the thought of it.

Dad, fortunately, came to my rescue. "Let's hold fire for a day or two. I'm sure there's no cause for concern."

"I'll give them another twenty-four hours," said Mum. "But that's as far as I'm prepared to go."

"I thought you weren't worried," I said.

"I'm not worried!" Mum tossed her head. "What should I be worried about? If Caitlyn's got in, you've got in. I just want things settled."

Fortunately the letter arrived the very next day. Just in time to stop Mum embarrassing me!

"So what does it say?" said Dad. "I'm on a knife-edge here!"

"It says she's been offered a place," said Mum. "What else would it say?"

"You tell me," said Dad. "All that fussing and fuming!"

"I wasn't worried," said Mum.

But I knew that she had been. Just for a little bit, Mum had actually had doubts. She had actually considered the possibility that I might not get in. It was a sobering thought. Did it mean Mum didn't have faith in me?

Fretfully I said, "If you'd let me go when I was eleven, I'd be in my second year by now. Why didn't you let me go then? Most people do!"

"Sean didn't," said Mum. "He didn't go till he was nearly fifteen."

I said, "Jen did!"

But Jen had got married and had a baby and given up dancing. That was practically a sin in Mum's book.

"Is it because of her you wouldn't let me?" I said. "Cos you were scared I'd do what she did?"

I'd once heard Mum and Dad discussing it and saying how maybe they'd made a mistake and pushed too hard. That maybe Jen's heart hadn't really been in it.

"I'd never give up just cos of having a baby," I said. "I don't even like babies all that much."

Dad said, "Hah! Famous last words… That's exactly what your mum used to say. And then she went on to have the three of you!"

"Yes, but I carried on dancing," snapped Mum.

"Until you had me," I said.

"You were an accident," said Mum. "But anyway, it was nothing to do with Jen giving up. If you want to know the truth, your dad and I weren't totally convinced that at the age of eleven you had the necessary discipline for full-time training."

I stared at her, indignantly. How could she say that? When I'd been dutifully attending classes three times a week for almost as long as I could remember! I hadn't ever grumbled or complained. Not even when she'd told me my arms were like waterlogged balloons or my fingers like bunches of sausages. In front of the entire class! I'd never resented it. Well, only a little bit. It had never stopped me trying to improve. I'd always worked hard; I'd passed all my exams. What more did she want?

"We just needed to make sure," said Mum, "that you were really committed. I've felt once or twice with Jen that maybe she was only going along to please me and your dad, because it was expected of her, and that perhaps if we'd held her back a bit she might have chosen a different path. We always knew with Sean that his heart was set on it. He only waited till he was older because boys can. There wasn't any particular rush. But thirteen is a perfectly good age! You don't have to look all reproachful. You've been accepted; you'll be starting in September. What's the problem?"

I said, "There'll be some people that have been there two years already!"

It would make me feel inferior. Everyone would know who my mum and dad were. They would wonder why I'd left it so late.

I'd never thought that way before; I'd always just accepted that I would go to ballet school when I was thirteen. I'd never really queried it. I hadn't had any idea that Mum and Dad were holding me back cos they didn't think I had enough discipline! It came as a bit of a shock, to be honest.

"You won't be the only one who's just starting," said Dad. "And let's face it, you couldn't have had any better training. Your mum may be a tyrant, but believe me, there'll come a time when you'll thank her for that!"

"Yes, and just think," said Mum, "if we'd let you go when you were eleven, you would never have met Caitlyn. We all know how much she owes you, but it's far from being a one-way street… It wasn't until you made her your pet project that you really started to show commitment. I was so proud when she took that audition with me and I knew that it was you who'd been teaching her… I couldn't have done a better job myself!"

I glowed. I couldn't help it! Mum almost never praises me. The most she'll say is, "That's a bit better." Not even better: just a *bit* better.

Dad caught my eye and winked. "Wonders will never cease, eh?"

"What wonders?" said Mum.

"Maddy knows! Don't you?"

I giggled and nodded. It was good, having Dad on my side.

"You and your little secrets," said Mum. She patted

my head as she left the room. "I think you'll find I always give praise when praise is due."

"So there you have it," said Dad. "If I were you, Mads, I'd go away and have a bit of a gloat... I'd say you deserve one!"

Chapter Three

It was our very first day at CBS. Caitlyn had begged me to wait for her at Waterloo so that we could walk there together. She'd said, "I know it's silly, but I'm all trembly." I hadn't teased her cos to be honest even I felt a bit of a quiver as we went in through the main entrance. We may have been coming to the school for almost a year for our extension classes, but we had only been visitors then. It was very different being full-time students. At last we could feel that we really belonged.

We'd spent the morning having registration, copying timetables and doing ordinary academic lessons – maths, English and geography, in this case – just as we would at any normal school. Now, at last, it was lunchtime. A group of us were sitting at a long table in the canteen, all eagerly looking forward to our first dance class of the day. There was me and Caitlyn, Roz and Alex, Tiffany Blanche, a tiny girl from Hong Kong called Mei, and Tiffany's friend Amber, whose surname I couldn't remember.

"Hey!" Tiffany suddenly leaned across and prodded me. "Maddy! *Why* was it again that you didn't come here at eleven, same as most of us?"

It was the second time she'd asked me. The first time I hadn't lowered myself to reply. I hadn't liked the way she'd asked the question! All superior, like anyone that was any good would have joined the school ages ago. What business was it of hers why I hadn't come when I was eleven? Now here she was, at it again, poking me, hoping to hear that I'd initially been turned down and had had to reapply.

You can tell with some people that they just want to score a point. I knew *why* she wanted to score a point. We'd hardly gathered for registration before Mei had recognised me and squeaked, "Oh! You're Sean O'Brien's sister! I saw your photo in a dance magazine!"

"Not just me," I said, hurriedly.

It had been all of us. Mum, Dad, me, Sean. Even Jen, who wasn't dancing any more. *Ballet's Royal Family* was what it had said. It had made me want to cringe. Caitlyn, needless to say, had been triumphant. She'd laughed and said, "Royal family... I told you so!"

I wished Mei hadn't seen it. *I* hadn't asked to be photographed. It's incredibly embarrassing when you're doing your best to be just another dance student and no different from anybody else. It hadn't bothered me at school when my friends had gone round boasting to everyone that "Maddy's family is *famous!*" They weren't actually famous, except in the ballet world, and no one at school had been particularly impressed. Being a ballet dancer isn't exactly the same as being a pop star. But now I was with people for whom ballet was the most important thing in the whole world. The last thing I wanted was to be singled out. I didn't mind them knowing who my mum and dad were, or that Sean was my brother. It wasn't like I was trying to keep it a secret. I couldn't have done, anyway. Almost everyone already knew. The dance world is quite small and Mei wouldn't be the only one who'd seen the photograph. But drawing attention to it had obviously got right up Tiffany's nose! And now she was getting right up mine. Was *I* the one who'd mentioned my family?

"I'd have thought," said Tiffany, dipping her spoon into her yoghurt pot, "that you wouldn't have wanted to waste any time. Personally I couldn't wait to get here!"

"Me neither." Amber nodded, eagerly. "I knew I wanted to come here right from the very beginning."

"Maddy knew from the very beginning that she *was* going to come," said Roz.

"So why didn't she?"

"What d'you mean, why didn't she? She has. She *is*. Isn't she?"

Roz stared round as if to say, *or am I seeing things?*

"She is *now*," said Amber.

"You surely must have been ready for it?" Tiffany was leaning forward again. A clump of yoghurt went splodging on to the table. "Oops!" She scooped it up and put it into her mouth. "I mean, it would be rather odd if you weren't."

I seethed, inwardly. I'd told Mum this would happen!

"I could have come earlier if I'd wanted," I said. I probably could have, if I'd nagged hard enough. It had just never occurred to me. I'd always been quite happy to wait till I was thirteen. Until now.

A wave of doubt suddenly engulfed me. Could it mean that Mum was right? That it wasn't until starting to teach Caitlyn that I'd developed a proper sense of commitment?

"You honestly didn't want to?" said Tiffany. She and

Amber exchanged glances. They shook their heads. *Unbelievable!*

"You probably didn't need to come earlier, did you?" said Mei. "Not if you had your mum to teach you."

"Yes, cos Maddy's mum," said Roz, "she's f—"

"Yeah, yeah!" Tiffany rocked back on her chair. "We all know who her mum is. *And* her dad. *And* her brother."

"This is what I'm saying," said Roz. "Maddy could have come here any time. But when you've got one of the best teachers in the world…"

I cringed. Mum *is* one of the best teachers. Roz was trying so hard to be loyal! But she was just making matters worse. And now Caitlyn was chipping in, as well.

"If anyone wasn't ready," she said, "it was me."

"Oh?" Tiffany's gaze immediately switched direction. "Why's that?"

"Cos I didn't even start learning till I was eleven."

"You didn't start *learning*?" Amber's gaze had also switched direction. It was like Caitlyn was some kind of creature from outer space, the way they were studying her.

Mei said, "That's amazing! You must have loads of natural talent."

"She has," I said.

"But I wouldn't be here if it weren't for you! It's all thanks to Maddy," said Caitlyn. "She was the one that believed in me. She gave me my first opportunity! *And* she was my first teacher." She giggled. "She was really strict! Not as strict as her mum, but she did used to bully me."

I said, "What cheek! I never bullied you."

"You did," said Caitlyn. "You were always lecturing me, saying how I didn't have any backbone. And then –" she turned back to the others – "you'll never guess what?"

"What?"

Everybody, now, was craning forward to listen.

"She made me learn her part for the end-of-term show at our school and right at the very last minute she went and twisted her ankle – *pretended* to twist her ankle – and said I had to go on instead cos I was her understudy. I've never been so terrified in my life. I was, like, shaking in my shoes!"

"Why?" said Tiffany. "What were you terrified of? That's what being an understudy's all about."

"So long as you knew the part," agreed Amber.

"She knew the part," I said. "She just wasn't properly trained. She'd never had a single lesson till I started teaching her. And I'd only been doing it for a couple of months! So going on in my place was incredibly brave, if you ask me."

"I'll say," said Alex, who'd heard the story before. "You wouldn't have got me doing it!"

"I didn't want to," said Caitlyn. "It was only cos of Maddy, bullying me."

"So what happened?" said Mei.

"What happened," I said, "was that she gave a totally brilliant performance and Sean saw it and told Mum and Mum said Caitlyn had better let her see what she could do, and as soon as she saw her she said she'd take her on."

"She gave me this special scholarship," said Caitlyn. "Cos she knew my mum couldn't afford lessons."

"That is so romantic," breathed Mei. "Like something out of a fairy tale!"

Tiffany said, "Hmm."

What did she mean, *hmm*? What was she implying?

"Mum doesn't take on just anybody," I said.

"I'm sure," purred Tiffany.

"It just helps," said Amber, "if you know the right people."

Earnestly Caitlyn said, "Yes, it does! I was just *so* lucky."

"It's the sort of thing," agreed Roz, "that will go in your biography."

"Oh," said Tiffany, "is someone going to do a biography of her?"

"Probably," said Roz. "When she's famous. They might even make a movie."

Tiffany looked at Roz with distaste. Then she looked at Caitlyn and her lip curled. I knew what she was thinking. How could someone so utterly ordinary ever hope to become famous?

It's true that Caitlyn isn't striking like Tiffany, with her long limbs and her blond hair. She isn't especially pretty, like Roz, and she doesn't have Mei's daintiness. It's only when she dances that she really comes alive. Offstage she can seem quite mouse-like and unremarkable. On stage she has what Mum calls star quality. It's not something that can be taught; you either have it or you don't. Sean has it, in buckets. By all accounts, Mum also used to have it. I am not sure that Jen did. I *hoped* that I might. I knew I came across, as they say. Across the footlights, that is. I don't just fade into the background. But whether I actually had star quality… Mum had never told me that I had. On the other hand, maybe she wouldn't. She'd never actually told Caitlyn; only said it to Dad one day, when she didn't realise I was listening.

"Do you know, I really think little Caitlyn might surprise us all… She definitely has potential."

"Star quality?" Dad had said, and Mum had said yes. "Star quality."

I couldn't help wondering if she'd ever said it about me. If she'd ever even thought it about me. Maybe it was just something she took for granted when it came to her own children. We were the O'Briens! Of course we had star quality.

Tiffany was still gazing at Caitlyn with a sort of amused contempt. "Famous!" she said, and gave a little snigger.

"D'you know," said Caitlyn, solemnly, "I've never even thought about being famous. Have you?"

She addressed her question to the table at large.

Alex said, "You'd better believe it! When I was eleven I used to spend hours interviewing myself… Alexandra Ellman, prima ballerina…"

"Oh, me, too!" agreed Roz. "I once interviewed myself as Roz Costello, Baby Ballerina… the youngest person ever to dance Princess Aurora… How pathetic was that!"

"I don't think it's pathetic," said Tiffany. "Perfectly natural, if you ask me."

"Exactly," said Amber. "What's the point of becoming a dancer if you don't believe you'll reach the top?"

Caitlyn hung her head. "I just never thought about it. All I wanted to do was dance."

"Didn't you ever have dreams when you were little?" said Mei. "When the curtain comes down and you're standing there, in the spotlight, and everyone's cheering and throwing flowers and someone gives you this enormous bouquet?"

"Not really."

"So what *did* you dream about?" said Amber.

"Mostly I just dreamt about being able to have ballet lessons… being able to buy a pair of ballet shoes and…" Caitlyn's voice trailed away, uncertainly.

I waited for either Amber or Tiffany to make one of their smart remarks. Tiffany half opened her mouth, then obviously thought better of it and snapped it shut again. Amber didn't even make the attempt. It was Roz who said, "That makes me feel really tawdry."

So then I said, "What does tawdry mean?" And Roz said she didn't really know, but it sounded right, and Alex said it meant sort of cheap, and we all agreed that maybe we shouldn't be worrying so much about becoming famous as about becoming the best dancers we possibly could.

Tiffany said, "Oh, how noble!" But it wasn't specially convincing.

At the end of the day we walked back to Waterloo together, the usual bunch of us – me, Caitlyn, Roz and Alex. Mei was with us for part of the way. As her family were in Hong Kong, she was staying in the hostel, just up the road, which the school kept for students who needed accommodation. Some were foreign, others simply lived too far away. Sometimes people's parents rented houses so that their mums – it was usually their

mums – could move to London to be with them. Quite often they let out rooms to other students. Amber, for instance, was living with Tiffany and her mum. I certainly wouldn't have wanted that, thank you very much – not with Tiffany! But I did think it might perhaps be fun to stay in the hostel rather than going back home every day. I suggested this to Caitlyn, as we left the others and peeled off towards the Underground, but she reacted with horror.

"What about my mum? She'd be all on her own!"

I said, "Yes, of course. I'd forgotten about your mum." Doing my best to sound sympathetic. I know that I am not always as understanding as I should be, though I do try to consider other people's feelings. I could see that it was difficult for Caitlyn. My mum is quite high-powered, totally preoccupied with her teaching. Plus she has Dad (when he is not flying about the world putting on his ballets) and also me. Not to mention Sean and Jen, who both live quite near and are for ever dropping by. Caitlyn's mum only has

Caitlyn, and is, I think, a rather shy and lonely sort of person.

"What will you do," I said, "when we have to go on tour?"

"You mean, if I get into the Company."

"Yes."

Caitlyn crinkled her nose. "I daren't look that far ahead! It's like tempting fate... Suppose I get thrown out?"

"Don't be silly," I said. "Of course you won't get thrown out! Don't even think about it."

"How can you help it?" wailed Caitlyn. "Everybody thinks about it!"

She didn't add, *everybody except you,* though she could have done cos it was quite true: I didn't think about it. Maybe I might nearer the time, but for goodness' sake we'd only just come to the end of our very first day!

"Someone told me," said Caitlyn, "that by the time we reach the end of our training there'll be only half of us left. And did you know –" she turned, big-eyed, to look at me – "did you know that six people were thrown out last term? Mei was telling me. *Six people!*"

"Pity it didn't include Tiffany," I said. "Can't think anyone would miss *her.*"

There was a pause. I could see Caitlyn struggling to think of something to say in Tiffany's defence. She is someone who always tries to see the best in people. I tend to just jump in and say whatever I feel.

"Don't tell me you *like* her?"

"She's a good dancer," said Caitlyn.

Grudgingly I said, "I suppose." From what little we'd seen. "I wish you hadn't told her about Mum giving you a scholarship, though."

"Why?" Caitlyn seemed startled. "Didn't you want me to?"

I said, "*I* don't mind. Not like it's a secret. But now she's going to go round telling everyone you only got in cos of knowing the right people."

"Oh." She bit her lip. "Maybe I did."

"That's absolute rubbish," I said, crossly. "Mum would

never have given you a scholarship if she didn't think you deserved it. As a matter of fact —" I wasn't sure that Caitlyn knew this — "it's the only scholarship Mum's ever given. *Ever!* Which just shows that she agreed with Sean. He was the one that said you had a special talent."

Predictably Caitlyn's face had turned bright pink, either because I'd mentioned Sean or because I'd told her what he'd said. Most likely a mixture of both.

I sternly informed her, not for the first time, that she really had to have a bit more faith in herself. "Otherwise," I said, "people like Tiffany will just walk all over you, like she tried to do today. She can try it with me as much as she likes. Doesn't bother me! You're too modest. It simply doesn't get you anywhere, not in this business. You have to be really tough in this business." (I was quoting Mum, here.) "If you keep putting yourself down all the time, people start thinking you can't be much good. It helps, of course, if you're naturally bumptious, which apparently I am, according to Sean."

Caitlyn giggled. "What's bumptious?"

"It's, like, when people are too full of themselves…
I know," I said, in an effort to be truthful, "that I can
sometimes be a bit pushy. But I'm never *nasty*. Not like
Tiffany. I'm not," I said, "am I?"

"Course you're not," said Caitlyn. "*She's* the one that's
full of herself."

Bitterly I said, "It's cos she started at CBS when she
was eleven. She reckons it makes her superior. Her and
that Amber!"

"But Mei started when she was eleven. She's not
superior."

"No," I said. "Mei's lovely."

"I'll tell you who else is nice… that girl Chloe."

"Chloe Adams?"

"Yes." Caitlyn nodded, enthusiastically. "Don't you
think she's nice?"

"She seems like she might be fun," I said. I hadn't had
much to do with her as yet.

"Actually," said Caitlyn, "she reminds me a bit of you."

"*Me?*"

How could she say that Chloe reminded her of me? We weren't in the least bit alike! The same height, maybe; but other than that we were about as different as could be. For a start, Chloe's hair was pale, like milky coffee, and very fine. My hair is thick and chestnut-coloured. Chloe was going to need a hairpiece when she was on stage. On the other hand, she did have this small elfin face with big dark eyes and cheekbones to die for. Every dancer dreams of having cheekbones! My face – I might as well be honest; there is no point in trying to hide from the truth – my face is what Mum once called *distressingly round*. I do have cheekbones, but I also, unfortunately, have cheeks. All plump and rosy and even, sometimes, covered in freckles. Great for comedy roles; but Giselle? Odette? Sleeping Beauty? I don't think so! Mum says briskly that there is always make-up, but who was ever going to cast me in those roles in the first place? They'd cast that blasted Tiffany. They'd cast Caitlyn. They'd probably cast Chloe.

Grumpily I said, "How can you think we're alike?"

"I didn't say you were alike." Caitlyn said it earnestly. "She just reminds me of you... Like this morning, when we had that lecture about nutrition and eating sensibly, and afterwards Chloe said she was going straight home to stuff herself with all the bad things she could find... crisps, and chips, and fudge, and—"

"She was only joking," I said.

"I know, it's just that it reminded me of you."

"You must be mad," I said. "I'd only have to *look* at a bit of fudge and I'd put on about five kilos."

"Well, I expect she would, too," said Caitlyn. "It's this jokey thing you do, pretending you don't really care when you obviously do. Like that time your mum wouldn't let you go for a sleepover at Liv's cos we had our intermediate next day and she said you couldn't afford to be up half the night; you needed to be well rested. D'you remember?"

I grunted. I sort of did.

"Livi said anyone would think you were planning on becoming a nun, the way your mum wouldn't let you go out and enjoy yourself like any normal person. She said you never seemed to have any fun at all. And you said—"

I said, "What? What did I say?"

"You did that thing that you do –" Caitlyn tossed her head – and said, *'I'm going to have all the fun I want! I'm not going to live like a nun!'*

I said, "Well, I'm not. Why should I? Sean doesn't!"

Caitlyn giggled. I said, "What's so funny?"

"Sean living like a nun!"

Crossly I said, "Like a monk is what I meant. He's always out partying! And I can't even begin to count the number of boyfriends he had before he met Danny!"

Maybe I shouldn't have said it, not that Sean would mind, but I felt this sudden urgent need to divert attention from myself. I did actually remember the sleepover incident. I'd argued quite fiercely with Mum about it and Mum had said –

I snapped my brain shut. I didn't want to think about what Mum had said!

"I'm just pointing out," said Caitlyn, "you made it sound like you thought having fun was more important than being a dancer. I knew you didn't really mean it! Like nobody really believes Chloe's actually going to cram herself with fudge. It's just her being her. Like it was just you being you."

You'll do well to buck your ideas up, my girl. That was what Mum had said. *You'll need to show a bit more commitment than that if you intend to get anywhere.*

I shifted, uncomfortably.

"Anyway," said Caitlyn.

I muttered, "Anyway what?"

"It's different for boys."

I thought, *Excuse me???* Normally I'd have ripped into her for that. I can't stand it when people say things are different for boys! Like boys can do whatever they want. Boys can get away with anything. Total sexist *rubbish*, if you ask me. But right at that moment I was quite relieved to change the subject.

"Talking of boys…" I said.

We talked of boys all the rest of the way. Caitlyn complained that she'd never really known any. I said that being at a girls' school I hadn't, either, apart from Sean, and I wasn't sure how much brothers counted.

"They've got to count for *something*," said Caitlyn.

"Well, we can make up for it now," I told her. "There's almost as many boys in our class as girls. It wasn't like that in Mum's day. In her day they found it really difficult to get boys into ballet. We're lucky!"

Very seriously Caitlyn said, "How did they manage to teach partnering?"

"Goodness knows," I said. "They must have used the same boys over and over till they got worn out! At least we won't have that problem. I'm really looking forward to starting on *pas de deux*!"

"Me, too." Caitlyn nodded, happily.

"Who d'you fancy?" I said.

She looked at me, alarmed.

"As a *partner*," I said.

"Oh! OK… Carlo, maybe?"

I said, "I knew you'd choose him!"

"Well, go on, then," said Caitlyn. "You choose!"

It kept us occupied for the rest of the journey. Far safer, I thought, than talking about me and my lack of commitment. Except that I really had only been joking! I was as committed as anybody. Caitlyn could see it; why couldn't Mum?

Chapter Four

My two best friends at Coombe House, before I left to go to ballet school, were Livi Samuels and Jordan Barker. The three of us had been really close. Caitlyn had only started at Coombe when she was eleven – when I *should* have gone to ballet school – and at first Livi and Jordan had been a bit resentful, cos of me suddenly spending so much time with Caitlyn, and Caitlyn and me having so much to talk about. I couldn't ever talk about ballet with Liv and Jordan, but until Caitlyn had arrived we'd been used to doing everything together so I could understand how they felt. They'd got over it after a while, though we'd never quite become a foursome. But the three of us had sworn to keep in touch and I'd promised faithfully that I would call them and let them know what it was like, being at ballet school full-time. I'd really meant to do so! It was just that things kept intervening and somehow or other the days had shot past without me even noticing until a whole fortnight had gone by, and in the end they'd decided that if I wasn't going to call them, they would have to call me.

"People keep asking about you," said Liv.

"Like, have we heard anything?" said Jordan.

"Even Miss Lucas! Just this morning. She said, '*I suppose you haven't heard how Maddy's getting on?*'"

"Well, you and Caitlyn, *actually*."

I said, "I'm really sorry; it's all just been so mad!"

"That's what Miss Lucas said. She said you were probably too busy."

That made me feel really guilty. Poor Miss Lucas! She'd always been so supportive. And I'd always been so impatient! I shouldn't have laughed about her the way I did. Just because she was getting on a bit and had these sentimental ideas about what dancing should be.

"All pink and pretty," as I'd once rather scornfully said to Mum.

Mum had told me off. She said that Miss Lucas was a sweet old soul and deserved my respect.

"Just remember your manners!"

I felt bad about it, now. Miss Lucas had put up with so much, simply because of who I was. That is, *Mum's daughter*. She was in awe of Mum. It even made her a little bit in awe of me. *Well, of course, Maddy*, she used to say, *you'll know far better than I do when it comes to performing*. And I'd been bigheaded enough to believe that I did!

Looking back, it made me feel ashamed. I had to remind myself that if it weren't for Miss Lucas and her eager enthusiasm, there would never have been any end-of-term production and Caitlyn would never have had the opportunity to show what she could do.

"I'll send her a card," I promised. "The Company has ones you can buy. I'll get something pretty! *Sylphides*, or something."

"She'd like that," said Jordan.

"Where are you both, anyway?" I said. "You sound funny!"

They giggled. "Mum and Dad are out," said Liv, "so we've put the phone on speaker. We're at my place, having a sleepover."

"We nearly asked you," said Jordan, "but we thought probably your mum wouldn't let you."

"She might have done," I said. "It's not like we have any exams coming up. On the other hand I do have to be in early for class."

"On a *Saturday*? Don't you have enough during the week? I should have thought you'd get sick of it."

"It's not all dancing," I said. "We have to do ordinary lessons as well. We have dance classes in the morning and dance classes in the afternoon, and all the ordinary stuff in between, same as at school."

"What d'you have to do that for?" said Jordan. "If you're going to be a dancer?"

I said, "Well, you need to know about art and music

and stuff. You have to be educated." *A fully rounded education* was what they called it.

"What about boys?" said Jordan. "Are there many boys?"

I said, "Loads of them!"

Over the speakerphone I heard two deep sighs.

"Imagine," said Liv, "you go off to ballet school and meet loads of them while we're stuck here at Coombe without so much as a single one in sight!"

"What are they like?" asked Jordan, eagerly.

What did she mean, what were they like? I said, "They're just boys, same as any others."

"They're not all gay, then? I thought they'd all be gay!"

Scornfully I said, "That's just a stupid myth. Not all boys that do ballet are gay. As a matter of fact," I added, "most of them aren't."

"Oh, well, of course, not *all*," agreed Jordan.

"Just some," said Livi, kindly.

They made it sound like they were humouring me. Like they thought they knew better than I did.

"If you're referring to Sean," I said, "just say so. It's not exactly a secret."

That shamed them into silence! For a few seconds they stayed quiet, obviously feeling rebuked. Then, brightly, Jordan said, "So how's Caitlyn?" Thus proving they *had* been referring to Sean. They both knew Caitlyn had this massive crush on him.

I said that Caitlyn was fine. I wasn't going to tell them she was already worrying about whether she would be kept on at the end of the first year. Most people probably did worry. There were just so many reasons for being rejected. More often than not for things you couldn't do anything about, such as growing too tall, or not being the right physical shape. You could be the most brilliant dancer in the world, but if you didn't fit the mould they wouldn't hesitate to get rid of you.

"Anyway," I said, "how is school? Tell me about school!"

They seized on it, thankfully. School was something we could all talk about. Livi told me how Ms Passmore had left to have a baby and how a *man* had taken her place.

"A real man!"

"Young," said Livi.

"Young-*ish*," said Jordan. She cackled. "Liv really fancies him!"

"I so do *not*," said Liv.

"You so do! I suppose at ballet school you have male teachers?"

"A few," I said. "Mostly at our stage they teach the boys."

"You mean you don't do classes together?"

"Not classical. We do character."

Livi started to say, "What's charac—"

But Jordan cut excitedly across her. "I must tell you, the funniest thing happened the other day. We were in morning assembly and this tiny little mouse suddenly appeared out of nowhere and guess what? Mindy Jacobs jumped on her chair and started screaming! Honestly it was hilarious!"

"I mean, *please*," said Livi. "She's a *prefect*."

"Naturally we didn't laugh at the time," said Jordan.

"No, cos that would have been unkind," agreed Liv.

"But *Mindy Jacobs*…"

They both went off into peals of giggles. I supposed it must have been quite funny; Mindy Jacobs had always been so desperately bossy and self-important. I was just finding it difficult to put myself back there, to remember how it felt, filing in to morning assembly, all the prefects sitting in a row down the side, all the rest of us bunched up in the middle. It suddenly all seemed so long ago and far away. My life now was so different. But I gave a bit of a giggle, to show willing.

"By the way," said Liv, "there's a new girl you'd be interested in. She's an ice skater."

"She's a bit like you," said Jordan. "She dances. Same as you, except on ice. Really clever! She's won medals. You really ought to meet her some time. You'd have loads to talk about!"

I said, "OK."

"Maybe when you're not so busy?"

"We could all get together," said Liv. "How about a Saturday afternoon?"

I said that a Saturday afternoon would be fine, so long as we didn't have any extra classes arranged.

"I'll give you a ring!"

This time, I thought, I really would. It wouldn't be right to drop old friends just because I'd made new ones, even if I did find it difficult to think of things to talk about. How could I tell them that just the other day Miss Hillier, one of our teachers, had had me out front, before the whole class, demonstrating my *pas de chat*? Livi and Jordan wouldn't understand how extraordinary it was, to be singled out. Plus they wouldn't have the faintest idea what a *pas de chat* was anyway. They thought ballet was all about being able to do the splits or lift your leg up over your head or spin like a top without getting dizzy. I mean, it *was* all of those things, but they were just, like, the basics. Like doing the splits, for instance, was good practice for when you came to do *grands jetés*. They weren't a proper step. And then all that silliness about boys that did ballet! It really made me ashamed of them. It just showed how our worlds had moved apart, and what a gulf there was between them. I could understand their world, cos I'd once belonged to it, but they didn't understand a single thing about mine.

I told Caitlyn, as we met up on Monday morning, that Jordan and Livi had rung. I told her how Miss Lucas had been asking after us, and that I was going to send her a card.

"Oh, please," begged Caitlyn, "can we send her one from both of us?"

I said, "I'll ask Sean to pick one out at the theatre. He can bring it round at the weekend. It's Mum and Dad's anniversary; we're all going out for a meal. Oh, and I told Jordan and Liv we'd get together some time. Maybe on a Saturday afternoon?"

"That's a good idea," said Caitlyn. "I'd like to see someone from school again. I s'pose everything's just the same?"

"Well," I said, "there's a new girl that does ice dancing, and Ms Passmore left to have a baby, and Mindy Jacobs got scared by a mouse and started screaming, and Jordan and Liv are green with jealousy cos of our being with boys."

Triumphantly Caitlyn said, "It's them that's living like nuns, not us!"

"Yes, and today," I said, happily, "we're starting *pas de deux*. I can't wait to see who we're partnered with!"

Caitlyn pulled a face. "I know I won't be with Carlo."

"You could be."

She shook her head. "I won't! I'm too short. They'll put him with someone taller. I just hope it's not Tiffany!"

I agreed that would be tiresome. Of course I knew *why* she'd picked on Carlo. He had black hair and brown eyes and a sort of look of Sean about him. She was so easy to read!

"Well, anyway," I said, "it'll be fun whoever they put us with."

In the end, it was Alex who got Carlo. I wondered if she had any idea that Caitlyn had wanted him. Or why! The boy I'd been hoping for was called Misha, who was actually English, but had been named after a famous Russian dancer called Mikhail Baryshnikov. I knew that he came from a ballet family, like me, and I thought that would have given us something in common. Unfortunately Mr Bishop, who took us for *pas de deux*, obviously had other ideas. He put Misha with Chloe and put me with a boy called Nico, which just at first was a bit of a disappointment cos I'd secretly quite fancied Misha. He was blond and classical-looking, like he'd be a natural for Siegfried or Prince Charming. What they called a *danseur noble*. Nico was small and compact and kind of cheeky-looking. More like Franz, from *Coppélia*. But then I was more like Swanilda from the same ballet rather than Odette or Giselle, so I had to accept that maybe

Mr Bishop knew what he was doing. By the end of class I had this feeling that Nico and I were going to get on well together.

Remembering what Sean had once said about partnering, how it made it all worthwhile if a girl bothered to show her appreciation for what you'd done, supporting her and showing her off to her best advantage, I took the opportunity to smile and say thank you. Nico at once grinned back and said, "thank *you*," and I went on my way feeling all buoyed up and exuberant. I was going to enjoy *pas de deux*!

"So what was all that in aid of?" said Tiffany, later, as we sat in the canteen at lunchtime. "What were you thanking him for?"

"I was just being polite," I said.

"But we hardly did anything! Not like there was any lifting."

"Just as well," said Amber, rather bitterly. "Goodness *only* knows why they put me with Oliver! He doesn't look like he could lift a rice pudding."

"Who would you have liked?" I said. "Carlo?"

"Carlo's lovely," said Alex.

Amber regarded her with distaste. "So aren't you the lucky one?"

"The whole point about partnering," said Tiffany, as if perhaps we weren't aware, "is that you should feel comfortable. If Amber doesn't feel comfortable, it's not going to work."

"So whose fault is that?" I said. "You have to give it time. You have to get used to each other. It's a *partnership*."

Tiffany rolled her eyes. "You don't say!"

"It's just as difficult for boys as it is for us. Sean always says that if you make mistakes, you make them *together*. You don't go round blaming the other person. He says if a girl holds her own weight and uses her own muscles to keep in position, it makes life a whole lot easier, cos otherwise, if she just lets go and expects the boy to do all the work, it doesn't matter if she's skinny as a rake, she can still feel like a sack of potatoes. Some girls," I said, "just treat their partners like they're a kind of machine. Sean says boys really hate it when they do that."

There was a pause. A few people nodded. Alex said, "Mm." Sort of doubtfully, like she wasn't too sure. Caitlyn was looking down at her plate.

"Well!" Tiffany smiled brightly at me across the table. "Thank you *so* much for the lecture, and for letting us have your brother's thoughts on the subject. We do all *know* he's your brother, by the way. You don't have to keep reminding us."

What on earth was her problem? I hadn't *been* reminding anyone. I hadn't even *said* that Sean was my brother. I'd just thought it would be interesting for people, knowing how boys felt. That was all!

At the end of the day, as we were on our way out, a handful of dancers from the Company appeared and began making their way up the stairs. The theatre was only just down the road, so occasionally, when their own studios were all occupied, the Company liked to borrow one of ours for last-minute rehearsals. We were quite used to seeing familiar faces. Even, sometimes, famous ones. Like last year, Mei had told us, she had actually caught sight of Alessandra Ferranti in one of the studios.

Ferranti was a big, big star, over from Milan for a special guest appearance. You didn't expect to encounter people that famous every day of the week. Today it was just a handful of minor soloists, plus Sean and Dana Martinu, his current partner. I guessed they'd come for a quick run-through of *Pulcinella*, which was a new short ballet being introduced into the repertoire.

"Hey, Sean!" I called out to him, up the stairs.

He turned, impatiently. "What?"

"You and Danny will be coming on Sunday, won't you?"

"Of course. Wouldn't miss it."

"In that case—"

"*What?*"

"Could you be very sweet and kind and bring one of the Company's postcards with you? Something pretty? For Miss Lucas? *Please?*"

He said, "Yeah, OK, if I remember," and disappeared with a bound up the last few steps.

Tiffany, following me and Caitlyn into the street, said, "Wow! That was *really* important."

I said, "Yes, it was, as a matter of fact."

"Sounded it," said Tiffany. And then she rolled her eyes at Amber, who rolled hers back, and they marched off together down the road.

"*Honestly,*" I said. "What is their problem?"

Caitlyn shook her head.

"What am I supposed to have done now?"

She sighed. "I don't know. Maybe…"

"What?"

"Maybe…"

I looked at her, through narrowed eyes. She was supposed to be on my side!

"Maybe *what?*"

"Maybe you shouldn't have called out to Sean like that?"

"Why shouldn't I call out to him? He's my brother!"

"But he's a member of the Company," pleaded Caitlyn. "He's one of their leading dancers."

"So what? He's still my brother! If I can't even talk to my own *brother*…"

Caitlyn bit her lip.

I said, "Oh, this is just stupid!" Reluctantly, though, I had to admit she might have a point. Lowly dance students didn't normally yell up the stairs at members of the Company, specially if they were one of the stars.

"All I wanted," I said, "was just to make sure he was going to be there on Sunday."

"You knew he was," said Caitlyn. "You already told me!"

I said, "Yes, well, he might have changed his mind. Something else might have turned up."

"Not when it's your mum and dad's wedding anniversary!"

"He leads a very busy life," I said. "I just needed to *know*. Cos of getting a card for Miss Lucas."

Caitlyn looked at me. The theatre is only just up the road. There wasn't any reason we couldn't have gone there ourselves and bought a card.

I said, "Oh, all right, in future I'll pretend I don't know him!" And then, very quickly, cos I was getting a bit bored with the subject, plus I really didn't see why I should be made to feel guilty, just for talking to my own brother, I said, "*You* could always come, if you like."

"On Sunday?" Her face lit up.

I said, "Yes! It'll be fun. We're all going out for a special meal."

"But isn't it just for family?"

"Not really," I said. "Danny's coming. And Steve."

Steve is Jen's husband. He's an accountant. Absolutely *nothing* to do with ballet. Danny at least is a photographer, who is known for his portraits of dancers.

"Shall I speak to Mum?" I said.

"Oh, Maddy, no!" She sounded horrified at the idea. "Your mum might think I was the one that had asked!"

"So I'll tell her you weren't. I'll tell her it was my idea. I don't see why Steve and Danny can come and not you."

"That's different! They *are* family. Please, Maddy, don't say anything to your mum!"

She was so agitated that I promised her I wouldn't, but in the end I did. I waited till we got home on Sunday night then said, "Could Caitlyn have come, if I'd asked?"

"Of course she could," said Mum. "Why didn't you?"

"Cos she begged me not to. She got all silly and shy and said she wasn't family."

"Well, no, but she's your friend and we all know her. You could have brought her along. It's a pity you didn't."

I said, "That's what I think. I think it would have been good for her. Seize every opportunity, that's what you once said. Otherwise she's going to miss out on so much! You know she's got this huge thing about Sean?"

Mum laughed. "Her and about a million others!"

I said, "Yes, it's pathetic. But she'd have been, like, in heaven, just being able to sit at the same table." Except, probably, she'd have been too covered in embarrassment to enjoy it.

"Never mind," said Mum. "You can take her backstage with you on Saturday. You're going to the matinee, aren't you? She can say hallo then. That'll make up for it!"

Chapter Five

"Alex wanted to know if we had anything exciting planned for the rest of the weekend," said Caitlyn, as we made our way to the Underground after Saturday-morning classes. "I didn't tell her we were going to the ballet."

"Why on earth not?" I said.

"Well, cos Tiffany was there, and you know how she gets."

I said, "Yes! All mean and jealous." Just because my *brother* had got tickets for us. What was so wrong with that? It was what anyone would do. It was what I would do, if I was in the Company. I'd get tickets for my family and friends. It would be very odd if I didn't, if you asked me.

I said this to Caitlyn. I said, "If you've got connections, it's stupid not to use them. You worry too much, that's your problem. But if you don't *want* to go and see Sean…"

A heartfelt squeak came out of her. "I do!"

"It's a bit ungrateful," I said. "When he goes to all this trouble."

Not that it was any trouble, not really. But he'd come up with the tickets all by himself. It wasn't like I'd had to beg for them. I hadn't been asking for favours!

"He got them for us specially," I said, "cos he knows it's one of my favourite ballets."

"*Love, the Magician?*" said Caitlyn. She sounded surprised.

"*El Amor Brujo*," I said. I like to use the Spanish title, not just to show that I know what it is and how to pronounce it – *El Amor Bruho*, not *Broojo*, as I once heard someone call it – but because I am a little bit in love with everything Spanish. *The Three-Cornered Hat* is another ballet I adore. Another is *Blood Wedding*. They are more my thing than Caitlyn's. She is mostly into the romantic and classical, like the first ballet we were going to see, *Masquerade*. *Masquerade* is one of Dad's earliest works and is what Mum calls "a froth". Very, very beautiful with gorgeous costumes, and music by Tchaikovsky. No storyline or drama; just pure dance. Exactly what Caitlyn likes best!

"Don't you care for *El Amor Brujo*?" I said.

"I don't know," said Caitlyn. "I've never seen it."

"Oh, you'll love it," I assured her. "Carmelo is one of the parts that made Sean's name!"

"I've read the storyline," said Caitlyn. "It sounds a bit complicated."

"It's quite simple, really," I said. "There's this young girl called Candela, who's in love with a handsome gypsy called Carmelo – that's Sean – but Candela's parents force her to marry someone else, who's unfaithful with a girl called Lucia, so Lucia's husband gets jealous and kills him, which means Candela's free to marry her sweetheart – that's Carmelo – except her dead husband starts haunting her and she does a *danza del terror* with his ghost – very scary! – and the only way to get rid of him is if they do a ritual fire dance, her and Carmelo. *Everybody* knows the ritual fire dance," I said; and I did a bit of it, there in the Waterloo Road, to show her. "You'll recognise it when you hear the music, it's brilliant!"

"So what happens?" said Caitlyn.

"Oh, well, it gets rid of the ghost! Lucia's spirited away by her dead lover—"

"Candela's husband."

"Yes. So Candela isn't haunted any more and she and Carmelo can finally be together and – well!" I took a deep breath. "That's it. I suppose it does sound a bit confusing, but—"

Caitlyn giggled.

"Just enjoy it!" I said.

"I will." Caitlyn gave a little hop and a skip. "I'm really excited!"

I was, too, though I'd never have admitted it. I'd

seen Sean dance a zillion times. I'd seen him in *El Amor Brujo* more than once. But this was the very first time I'd ever been to the theatre on my own, without either Mum or Dad, or Jen; so even though it was an afternoon performance, which I never think is quite as thrilling as an evening one, it still felt like a special occasion.

"Look," I said. "Dad lent me his opera glasses... You can use them, if you want. Like if you want close-ups of people."

She blushed at that. She knew what I meant by people!

"Here." I pushed them at her. "I don't need them."

"Maybe I won't, either," said Caitlyn, bravely.

"You might as well," I said. "We're quite a way back."

The Millennium Hall, where City Ballet perform, is almost like a second home to me; I've been going there almost ever since I can remember. Up until quite recently Mum used to refer to it as "the new place", which always amused me cos I wasn't even born till after the Millennium. Back in Mum's day, the Company had used an old music hall theatre in the East End. Mum always said it was "very historical, very uncomfortable". The Millennium Hall is bright and modern. City Ballet shares it with the London Players, who are a theatre company. It has a big stage for large-scale works, such as *Swan Lake* or *Sleeping Beauty*, or if the Players put on a musical or maybe some Shakespeare, and a smaller one for more intimate works. It also has a couple of studios which people can use for experimental pieces, or sometimes poetry recitals or musical evenings.

Seen from outside, the building looks a bit plain and boring, but inside it is quite magical. It has this huge foyer with a wide staircase going down to the main auditorium, and photographs of actors and dancers covering the walls. Not just present-day people, but what Dad calls "stars of yesteryear", as well. There's several of Mum, all young and sparkling, in various ballets. My favourite is Mum as the Firebird. There are also a couple of Dad, one as an Ugly Sister in *Cinderella* and one as the Showman in *Petrushka*. Not very romantic, but Dad mainly stuck to character roles. He was always more interested in choreography than in dancing. There are loads of Sean, of course, and if you looked hard enough you could even find one of Jen, as the Fairy of the Crystal Fountain in *Sleeping Beauty,* one of the very last roles she danced.

Just as I had predicted, Caitlyn and I were seated high up in the gallery, which I think is actually the best place for ballets like *Masquerade* as it means you can see all the patterns made by the dancers, though maybe it's not quite so good for dramatic works, where sometimes you feel it would be good to be a bit closer. I whispered encouragingly to Caitlyn that she should use Dad's opera glasses. I think she was quite grateful to be given permission!

"So what did you think?" I said, as the curtain came down at the end of *El Amor Brujo*. "Did you like it?"

"It was amazing," she breathed. The expression on her face was one of pure bliss. I felt a giggle bubbling up and sternly suppressed it. She had had Dad's opera glasses glued to her eyes practically the whole time! But it is not fair to laugh.

"Which did you like best?" I said. "*El Amor Brujo* or *Masquerade*?"

"Oh! Well… they're so different," said Caitlyn.

"But which one would you rather be in, if you could choose?"

I could see her struggling. She sighed. "It doesn't really matter which one I'd rather be in cos nobody is ever going to cast me as Candela. They're not," she said, "are they?"

I had to agree that they probably weren't.

"They will you," said Caitlyn. "It's your sort of part!"

"Like Giselle is yours," I said. "That's what you'll be cast as."

She looked at me, doubtfully. "Do you really think so?"

I thought, *For goodness' sake!* I felt like telling her to stop being so humble. She must know she was dead right for Giselle! Apart from anything else, I'd told her so before. Lots of times.

I jumped up. "Let's go see Sean!"

"What, in his dressing room?"

"Yes!"

She hesitated.

"So are you coming," I said, "or not?"

"You go," said Caitlyn. "I'll wait for you in the foyer."

In the end I left her to it; you just can't help some people. I felt that if I had a crush on someone I'd jump at the chance to be near them. I certainly wouldn't get all silly and embarrassed and hide myself away. She really had to make more of an effort if she wanted to get anywhere. I couldn't see Tiffany turning down an invitation to go backstage and talk to one of the stars, even if she did resent him being my brother. She'd be there like a shot! Tiffany was someone who knew instinctively that you had to seize every opportunity. I didn't much like her, but I didn't blame her for being ambitious. Caitlyn might be a far worthier person, and even, probably, a better dancer, but you needed a bit more than that if you wanted to get noticed.

There was a whole load of people in Sean's dressing room. If Caitlyn had been with me, I'd have wormed my way through, dragging her with me, but Danny was there, and he smiled and came over when he saw me, so I talked to him, instead.

"Where's Caitlyn?" he said. "Didn't she come, after all?"

I said yes, she was waiting for me in the foyer.

"She was too shy to come round and say hallo. Not that she'd have had much chance, anyway."

Danny said, "No, it's a bit crowded, isn't it? Do you want to hang on here, or shall we go back out front and find her?"

"Might as well," I said. "Tell him I came round – oh, and tell him he was brilliant... as usual!"

"Will do."

"So who are all these people?" I said, as we closed the door behind us.

Danny pulled a face. "Don't ask me! You know Sean…
he's like a magnet."

"Well, so long as it keeps him happy," I said.

"Oh, he thrives on it! The more the merrier. Still, I
guess it's what it's all about… being a performer. Where
would you all be without your adoring public?"

"Well, but it's the same for you," I said. "I know
you're not a *performer*, but it must make you feel good
when people admire your photographs."

Danny said, "Yes, and guess what? I've been
commissioned to do a photoshoot for a new ballet
book… *The Lives of Young Dancers*. All the way from
first year right through to graduation. It's going to be
centred on your school, so I'll be paying a visit some
time to sort out the details."

"Sounds exciting," I said.

"It should be fun."

"Will you be using lots of us, or just one or two?"

"I thought probably I'd concentrate on one boy and
one girl from each year, plus lots of general stuff…

classes, rehearsals, performances. That sort of thing. What d'you think?"

What I immediately thought was that if he was planning to choose me, from my year group, Tiffany was going to go completely ballistic. She would never let me live it down.

Just because he's friends with your brother…

It even crossed my mind, just for a second, that maybe I should ask him *not* to choose me. He was almost certainly going to. After all, he *was* Sean's boyfriend and that did make him almost a member of the family. It was only natural to help members of your family, even if some people did think it wasn't quite fair. But then again, why should it bother me what people thought?

If you've got connections, it's stupid not to use them.

Wasn't that what I'd said to Caitlyn that very afternoon? It would be *utterly* stupid if I turned down the chance to appear in Danny's book. What did I care about Tiffany and her raging jealousy? She certainly wouldn't hesitate if she was the one with connections, so why should I?

Danny and I walked back up the steps together and into the foyer. I didn't immediately spot Caitlyn. I thought probably she would be in the shop, browsing among the books and the postcards, but then suddenly I caught sight of her. I froze. "*Omigod!*" I said.

Danny said, "What?" Then, following the direction of my outraged gaze, he added, "Oh! There she is."

She was standing in front of Mum's *Firebird* photo. Not just standing: *posing*. Mum's mirror image. Heads were turning as people walked past. A woman with two small girls had stopped to watch. The girls were staring, mouths agape, eyes wide with wonderment. I made a dart forward, but Danny put out a hand and held me back.

"Let me just…" He pulled out his camera. Danny never goes anywhere without his beloved camera. "There! Got it! That," he told me, "is a near perfect picture."

★ 97 ☆

But she shouldn't have been doing it! Not in the foyer of the Millennium Hall. Not in any public place. Madam would be furious!

I said this to Danny, who was still snapping away. I have noticed this before, with professional photographers: they simply never know when to stop.

"What's the problem?" said Danny. "What's she doing that's so wrong?"

"It's very bad manners," I said.

You just don't do that sort of thing! You might when you were a little bratty five-year-old, showing off. Not when you were one of Madam's students.

"It's *Firebird*," said Danny, "isn't it?"

I said, "Yes, it is, and she ought to know better!" Firebird wasn't her part anyway. Even if it was, that was no excuse. It was as bad as leaving the theatre without removing your make-up. It just *wasn't done*.

"Don't be mad at her," urged Danny. "I'm sure she doesn't mean to upset anyone."

She had upset *me*. I was the one responsible for her!

I went marching determinedly across the foyer, but too late: she was already engaged in earnest conversation with the mum and the two little girls. I arrived just in time to hear the mum say, "Would it be awful cheek to beg a selfie? They'd be so thrilled! Wouldn't you, girls?"

The two little girls both nodded, eagerly. The way they were staring at Caitlyn you'd have thought she was already a star. Blushing, Caitlyn protested that she was still only a student.

"But just think," said the mum, "when you're famous they'll be able to tell everyone that they met you when you were still at ballet school!"

Oh, I thought, *yuck.*

Caitlyn gave a little embarrassed giggle. "That's if I ever get famous," she said. And then she caught sight of me and Danny and a look of relief came over her face.

"This is my friend Maddy," she said. "Maddy O'Brien… She's a dancer, too. Would you like to take a photo of her as well?"

One of the little girls squealed. "You're Sean O'Brien's sister! I saw a picture of you!"

Caitlyn smiled hopefully at me. "Maddy?"

Not the least idea that she'd done anything wrong! But I dutifully lined up next to her, wiped the scowl from my face and forced myself into a gracious smile. I was really cross with Caitlyn, but I knew I couldn't take it out on the two girls. It wasn't their fault; they were just a couple of excited little ballet fans. You had to respect your fans. Mum had always drummed it into me.

Just remember… you're nothing without them!

"Well," said Danny, as we went back across the foyer. "How flattering was that?"

"Wasn't flattering at all," I muttered.

"Way to get noticed, eh?"

"I didn't mean to get noticed," said Caitlyn, earnestly. "It was really embarrassing!"

"Yes," I said, "it was. You're lucky someone like Miss Hickman didn't catch you."

"Oh, come on," said Danny. "No harm done. You

made two little girls very happy, and they are not the only ones –" he patted his camera – "to have got some brilliant photos!"

Chapter Six

I tried to work out, afterwards, what it was that had made me so cross with Caitlyn. It really hadn't been such a huge crime as all that; I knew she hadn't been showing off. *Hey, everybody, look at me!* Caitlyn wasn't like that. If she was too shy to come back and say hallo to Sean, she was certainly too shy to draw attention to herself in a crowded foyer. To do it deliberately, that is. She'd obviously been studying Mum's picture and had fallen into the same pose almost without realising it.

I was glad, now, that I hadn't had a go at her. I would have done if it hadn't been for Danny. I wondered if he had told Sean about it – whether he'd shown him the photos he'd taken. Sean would probably have laughed, if he'd been there. He's always been what Mum calls *irreverent*, meaning he tends to make fun of rules and regulations and of anyone in authority. He's one of the few people, Mum says – not altogether approvingly – who's been known to pull Madam's leg and get away with it. I just hoped Danny hadn't told him how cross I'd been, cos that would make me sound like some kind of self-righteous nag.

I wasn't a nag! Sometimes, like Sean, I am even a bit *irreverent*. It was Danny's fault if I'd got cross. The way he'd reacted, like he'd suddenly seen this vision. Like Caitlyn was all set to become the next Darcey Bussell, or something. I mean, what did he know? He wasn't a dancer! Just because he lived with Sean didn't make him some kind of expert. Caitlyn hadn't been doing anything the rest of us couldn't. Not that the rest of us *would*. Well, I wouldn't! I'd know better. I really thought Caitlyn should have done, too.

A couple of days later, she broke it to me: she was going to be one of the dancers featured in Danny's book.

Just at first, I couldn't believe it. He'd chosen *Caitlyn*, rather than me? I'd been so sure he was going to choose me! He *had* been going to. I knew he had! Until he'd caught sight of her, posed in front of Mum's photo, and suddenly – wham! – he'd had a change of heart. A *near perfect picture*. That was what he'd said. In other words, Caitlyn was actually being rewarded for her shocking display of bad manners!

It was what I thought, too, but I could hardly admit it. I said, "What makes you think that?"

"Cos you're family! It's like you said… when Sean got us tickets. You said it was what anyone would do."

"That was just tickets," I said. "This is *work*. You have to be professional when it comes to work. Like if Dad puts Sean into one of his ballets there's always going to be people that'll say, '*Oh, it's just because he's family.*' It actually isn't, cos Sean's a good dancer; but it's still what people would say. Some people."

Caitlyn's face suddenly cleared. "Of course! That's why Danny couldn't use you… It's not really fair, though, is it? Just cos of people like Tiffany getting jealous."

I struggled for a moment. I like to be honest whenever I can. "It's not *just* because of people like Tiffany," I said. "Danny's an artist. Like Dad. Artists always put their work above all else. In the end they choose whoever they think is best."

Caitlyn munched uncertainly on her lower lip. A slight frown creased her forehead. I could tell exactly what she was thinking. *Is Maddy really saying I'm the best?*

I struggled a bit more. I was trying all I could not to sound bitter or resentful, but I have to admit I didn't really believe Caitlyn was any better than I was. If as good. Not being bigheaded, but I was the one that got chosen to demonstrate my *pas de chats*, not Caitlyn! It was probably right, what she'd said. In spite of being an artist and putting his work above all else, Danny must have felt it wouldn't be right to use me, no matter how much he might want to. It wasn't the same as Dad using Sean in his ballets. Dad really *did* have to choose the best person. But really, when it came to it, just posing for a book of photos was hardly the same as actually dancing. Nowhere near as important! Just so long as Caitlyn was aware of it.

"If you want to know the truth," I said, "it's probably those pictures he took of you the other night." I might have added, *when you were making a spectacle of yourself in a public place.* But I spared her. "I reckon that's what decided him. Like why bother looking for anyone else when he'd already got you?"

"Mm." She nodded, slowly; digesting the idea. "If he'd come and watched us in class he'd probably have chosen someone quite different… like Tiffany, for instance. That would be even worse," she said, "wouldn't it?"

I said, "Worse than what?"

"Worse than not being able to use the person he really wanted cos of what people might say!"

Well, yes, I thought, *it would*. Tiffany would be totally impossible. Caitlyn was at least humble. But I still couldn't help feeling hard done by. It wasn't right that people should be rewarded for behaving badly. Stupidly, as well, cos it *had* been stupid, getting all silly and shy and not coming backstage to see Sean. It really is very annoying, the way things sometimes work out.

Later that night, in my bedroom, I stood in front of the full-length mirror on my wardrobe door and studied myself. Dancers are always studying themselves in full-length mirrors. It's not a vanity thing, it's because we're always on the lookout for faults. Am I properly turned out? Is my bum tucked in? Are my shoulders relaxed?

I drew myself up in the Firebird pose. Firebird was *so* my part! Surely by now Danny must have learnt enough about ballet to realise that Caitlyn wouldn't be chosen to dance it in a million years? Sean would know. I couldn't believe he wouldn't have said something! *"Very pretty picture, but of course she's quite wrong for the part."*

I looked at myself more closely. My eyes narrowed. Was that a roll of fat where my hip ought to be?

I pinched at it. Was it? Or was it just my imagination? Dancers are always imagining they are putting on weight. It's like an occupational hazard. But if it was a roll of fat...

That would explain why Danny hadn't chosen me! Danny was an artist; he had the eye of a professional photographer. He'd have homed straight in on it.

It was, in its way, a relief – nowhere near as bad as Danny not choosing me cos he thought Caitlyn was better. Which, if I was to be honest, had still been my secret fear. But weight? Weight was nothing! Weight could be got rid of just as easily as it could be put on.

Now that I had identified the problem, I didn't intend losing any time. I am one of those people. I know better than to starve myself. *Eat sensibly;* that is what they are always drilling into us. We had all heard the tale of the student from a few years back, who had actually been a friend of Jen's. She'd been so desperate to keep her weight down that she'd gone on a strict diet of bottled water and celery and had dramatically passed out in the middle of class. What was so sad, Jen said, was that she'd always been terrified of being thrown out.

"And then they went and threw her out anyway. She was devastated."

That poor girl had become almost a legend. She was always being held up as a dire warning; though Jen always said that it was the school that was to blame.

"It's like a reign of terror from the moment you get there… They keep you living on a knife edge."

It's true that most of us do live in constant fear of the physical assessments we have to go through. You wait to hear the dreaded words: too tall, too short, too fat, too thin… You can never relax for a moment. Even I, who am not at all an anxious kind of person, can get a bit stressed around assessment time.

That afternoon at the end of our *pas de deux* class with Mr Bishop, I suddenly heard myself asking Nico whether he thought I was too heavy. The words just came shooting out of my mouth, with no warning.

Nico's cheeks turned brick red. "Are you saying you don't think I'll be strong enough to lift you?"

"No!" Now I'd gone and upset him. We'd been getting

on so well! Why did I have to open my stupid blabbering mouth? "Honestly," I told him, "I didn't mean that at all! I just meant —" I lowered my voice to a whisper — "I'm scared I'm getting fat!"

Nico ran his eyes over me. *All* over me. I tried not to shrink into myself.

"You don't look fat," he said. "What's more important, you don't *feel* fat. I'd know if you were gaining weight. I'm your partner. Trust me!"

I wanted to, but how could he be so certain? We hadn't even started doing lifts yet! He had no idea how heavy I was.

Nico grinned. "You think I wouldn't notice if you were putting it on? I'd know immediately." He placed his hands either side of my hips. "See? I'd be the first to feel it!"

I told myself that of course he was right. Being partners is a very intimate relationship: if Nico thought I was getting fat he'd find some way of letting me know. Not straight out, maybe; just little hints every now and then until I'd picked up on the message. It still didn't stop me peering sideways at myself in a plate-glass window as Caitlyn and I walked back together, later on, to the Underground. Once you get it into your head that you are becoming huge and gross and horrible it is very difficult to give up on the idea. It quickly becomes an obsession. I even, almost, turned to Caitlyn and asked her. The only reason I didn't was that it would have been too shaming. But I still wasn't totally convinced!

I arrived home just as Sean was on his way out. He raised a hand as he shot past me down the hall. I called after him: "Hey, Sean!"

"What?"

"Can I ask you something?"

"Only if it's quick, I'm in a rush."

"It is quick! I just want to know—" I took a deep breath. Sean would tell me the truth, if anyone would. He wouldn't spare my feelings.

"*Well?*" He was waiting, impatiently, one hand on the door.

"It's just—" The words came gabbling out of me. "*Doyouthinkl'mgettingfat?*"

"Oh, for goodness' sake!" He rolled his eyes. "Don't be so narcissistic!"

I opened my mouth to say, "What's that supposed to mean?" but thought better of it. He obviously wasn't in the mood. But I had to know!

"Does Danny think I am?"

He nearly exploded at that. "How the hell should I know what Danny thinks?"

"Well, like, if he's said anything." Like, *I would have asked Maddy to be in my book, but she's getting so heavy.* "Has he said anything?"

Sean wrenched the door open. "You think we don't have more important matters to talk about than my self-obsessed little sister?"

I said, "I'm not self-obsessed, I'm worried! And what's… whatever it was… narciss-stic anyway?"

"Narcissistic! Look it up."

"I can't, I don't know how to spell it."

"So find out!"

The door slammed behind him. I was left by myself, feeling hurt. It wasn't like Sean to be so short-tempered. He may be a big star and used to people worshipping him, but he is always approachable. I couldn't understand what I'd done to upset him; all I'd wanted was his honest opinion. He didn't have to bite my head off!

I found Mum and Dad downstairs in the kitchen and grumbled to them about it.

"What's Sean's problem? Why is he in such a hateful mood? He's just practically bitten my head off!"

"No doubt you gave him good cause," said Dad.

"I did not!" I said it indignantly. "All I did was just ask him a simple question. He didn't have to snap at me."

"Don't be too hard on him," said Mum. "You caught him at a bad moment."

I said, "*Oh?*" I didn't know Sean ever had any bad moments. It seemed to me he just sailed through life.

"Apparently," said Mum, "he and Danny have had some kind of falling-out so he's feeling a bit raw."

Aggrieved, I said, "Well, he could have told me! Why couldn't he just tell me? *'I'm sorry I can't take much interest in you and your stupid little problems right now; I have enough problems of my own.'* That was all he had to say. Then I'd have understood."

"You really think that sounds like Sean?" said Mum.

"Well, he told you and Dad!"

"So now we're telling you. What was your stupid little problem, anyway? Can we be of help?"

I mumbled that it wasn't important. Mum would go totally ballistic if she thought I was getting obsessed with my weight. She has this thing about dancers who let themselves get too thin. "Like watching a stage full of coat hangers!" On the other hand she also has a thing about dancers who let themselves get *fat*.

"Who wants to see a load of beach balls bouncing about?"

Best not say anything. She'd only start lecturing.

"So how are you getting on with Chris Bishop?" said Dad.

He meant Mr Bishop who took us for *pas de deux*. I'd forgotten he and Dad had been in the Company together. There was almost no one on the staff that Mum and Dad hadn't either danced with or been taught by.

I told Dad that I was really enjoying Mr Bishop's classes.

"This boy I'm dancing with? Nico? It's like we just instinctively understand each other."

Well, we *had* understood each other, before I'd gone and upset Nico by asking him if he thought I was too heavy. It was a really thoughtless thing to have done; I saw that now. Boys are every bit as sensitive as girls. I knew from Sean that they worry just as much, for instance, about their height and their upper-body strength as we do about disappearing hip bones or bulging thighs. It was one occasion when I really wished I'd thought before opening my mouth.

"I'm glad you're enjoying it," said Mum. "If you don't

get on with your partner, it can make life really miserable. You want to hear Sean on the subject!"

The mention of Sean reminded me. I said, "What does narsss-is-ist mean?"

Mum raised an eyebrow, like, *what has that to do with anything?*

"I just suddenly thought of it," I said. "What's it mean?"

"Narcissist? It comes from a Greek myth about a beautiful young man called Narcissus and a nymph called Echo, who falls in love with him."

"That's the Roman version," said Dad. "In the Greek version it's a young man who falls in love with him."

"Whatever," said Mum.

"I'm telling you," said Dad.

I said, "So what happens?"

"Oh! Well, in either version," said Dad, "he happens to catch sight of himself in a lake—"

"A pool, actually," said Mum.

"Lake, pool, what does it matter?" Dad was starting to sound a bit irritable. He hates it when people keep interrupting. "Pond, puddle, river... the point is that he sees his reflection and is so entranced by his own beauty that he falls in and drowns."

"Which he could hardly do in a puddle," said Mum.

"So what does it mean," I said, "if you actually *call* someone a narciss...ist?"

"It just means they're a bit too self-regarding."

I thought, *That is so unfair*! Dancers have to be self-regarding. We do nothing *but* regard ourselves. All of us. Including Sean. If I was a *narcissist*, so was he!

"Know what?" I said, as I turned to go back up the stairs. "I bet it wasn't Danny."

Mum looked puzzled. "You bet what wasn't Danny?"

"Him and Sean breaking up... I bet you anything you like it was Sean!"

Chapter Seven

I said it again next day when I was breaking the news to Caitlyn.

"I bet it was Sean!"

Caitlyn looked at me reproachfully. "What makes you think that?"

"Cos he's my brother," I said, "and I know what he's like… too used to getting his own way. *And* he's spoilt."

"How can you be so horrible?" cried Caitlyn.

She was bound to defend him. When you have an enormous crush on someone you can't ever accept they have any faults. I love Sean dearly, but he is not a saint. Far from it!

"I'm just telling it like it is," I said.

"*You* don't know what happened," said Caitlyn.

No, I didn't. But I was thinking back to the other night, in Sean's dressing room. Filled to the brim with a chattering horde of friends and admirers. What was it Danny had said?

You know Sean… he thrives on it! The more the merrier.

But he'd pulled a face as he'd said it. What if Danny wasn't so keen on that way of life? Speaking for myself, I reckon I might quite like it. Posh parties, late-night suppers after the show, throngs of adoring fans clamouring for my autograph… *Yesss!* My sort of thing! On the other hand, I do accept it might not suit everyone. Danny was very different from Sean; Sean had always been madly sociable. Mum used to say if he wasn't careful he would burn himself out. Not that he ever took the least bit of notice. Sean never takes any notice of anyone; just does his own thing, regardless. So if Danny would rather they had a life that was a bit more private, too bad!

★ 119 ☆

I could *sort* of see it from Sean's point of view. It is incredibly demanding, being a dancer. Even if you are one of the stars you still have to have class every day. And then there are rehearsals, and costume calls, and interviews, and photographs, not to mention constant physio sessions for all the aches and the pains and the pulled muscles that dancers are never free from. And that is *without* the actual performances several times a week. It wasn't any wonder Sean felt the need to go a bit wild in his time off. I felt sure I would be exactly the same.

I tried explaining some of this to Caitlyn. "Nobody can be disciplined *all* of the time – well, most people can't. Mum says *she* was. Madam probably was. But Sean doesn't work that way."

"So what you're saying is," said Caitlyn, "it's not *his* fault, it's just him and Danny wanting different things."

"Yes! Well – maybe."

"Don't you think that's sad?" said Caitlyn.

I did think it was sad cos I really loved Danny. We all

loved Danny! He was like one of the family. Mum had always said he was good for Sean on account of being a bit older and a whole lot more sensible — which is something Sean isn't. But I did think Sean could at least have given way a little. Like just going a *bit* wild, every now and then. He didn't have to do it every single night!

"Know what?" I said. "I reckon you ought to go and talk to Danny."

"Me?" She recoiled, in horror. "I couldn't talk to Danny!"

I said, "Why not? He won't mind. You're in favour at the moment."

"But it isn't any of my business!"

"I thought you said it was sad?"

"It is, but it's between him and Sean."

"Yes, and left to themselves they'll never get anywhere!"

"Maybe you could talk to him," said Caitlyn. She looked at me, pleadingly. "You've known him a lot longer than I have."

"Not that much longer," I said, "and anyway, I'm not the one in favour. You're the one he's putting in his book. Some people," I said, "might even think you owe him."

I could see from the expression on her face – what I call her Dying Swan look – that I'd succeeded in making her feel a bit guilty, but still she wouldn't budge. She just kept shaking her head and saying she couldn't; it was between him and Sean.

When I got home I found Dad downstairs in what we call the family room. Half of it's kitchen and half of it is where we eat and chill out. I said, "Dad?"

Dad said, "Maddy?" He was sprawled on an old sofa, drinking coffee.

I sank down next to him. "Dad," I said, "Can I ask you something?"

"Ask away!"

I don't usually go to Dad with problems as he is not very good at solving them. He is good at making ballets, but he is not really a people person – and this was definitely a people problem. But Dad was the only person there so I took a breath and plunged in.

"It's about Sean," I said.

"What about him?"

"I think he's behaving like an idiot!"

"How surprising," said Dad. "What's he done now?"

"Him and Danny," I said.

"Oh. That," said Dad.

What did he mean, *oh that*? Like it wasn't anything important. This is what happens when you try to speak to Dad. He doesn't understand. He is not at *all* a people person.

"I think someone ought to talk to him," I said.

"You do?"

I nodded.

"And what would someone say?"

"Tell him to apologise, maybe?"

"Tell Sean to apologise?" Dad raised an eyebrow at me over his coffee mug. "And what do you think that would achieve?"

"It's what I did one time," I said. "When me and Livi

had this terrible row and stopped talking. It went on for, like, ever and it was just *so* miserable I couldn't bear it so in the end I went and said sorry, and she said sorry, and we kissed and made up and—"

"You think that's what Sean should do?"

I said, "Yes!"

"And you really believe that if you tell him, he'll go and do it?"

I said, "Yes! Well… he might."

"Who might what?" said Mum, suddenly appearing at the bottom of the steps.

Dad shook his head. "Sean might say sorry and he and Danny might kiss and make up."

"Really?" said Mum.

"They might if someone goes and talks to Sean." I said it eagerly. Surely Mum would understand?

"She's worried about him," said Dad. "She thinks he's behaving like an idiot."

"He probably is," agreed Mum. "It wouldn't be the first time."

"But, Mum," I said, "it's making him unhappy!" He would never have snapped at me if he hadn't been unhappy. I didn't like it when Sean snapped at me.

"Oh, Maddy, I know it's sad," said Mum, "but these things happen. It's all part and parcel of human relationships."

Dad set down his coffee mug. "'*The course of true love never did run smooth*…' That's Shakespeare," he said. "*A Midsummer Night's Dream.*"

"A *stupid* play!" I said it crossly. I didn't want to talk about *A Midsummer Night's Dream*. I wanted to talk about Sean and Danny.

"It makes a good ballet," said Dad.

"A very good ballet," said Mum. "It's about time the Company staged a revival."

"Either that or I do a totally new version."

"That's always a possibility. Who would you have in mind for Oberon? Do you think Sean's weighty enough?"

"Not sure it's his part. I'd have thought maybe one of the lovers?"

"Mm." Mum thought about it. "That might work. And then you c—"

"*Mum!*" I screamed it at her.

"What?" She spun round. "Oh, yes, you wanted to talk about Sean… Quite honestly, sweetheart, I'd just forget about it, if I were you. He's a big boy. Quite old enough to manage his life for himself. I doubt he'd thank any of us for interfering." She turned back to Dad. "I take it you wouldn't try to cover the whole play? I mean, would you be thinking two acts or just condensing into one?"

I made an angry noise, but already they were too busy planning Dad's version of *A Midsummer Night's Dream* to notice. I don't think they even noticed when I went pounding noisily back up the basement steps. What was the *matter* with them all? Was I the only one who cared? *Maybe*, I thought, *I should ring Jen. She* was a people person!

I shut myself away in my bedroom and called her number. She answered at once, sounding bright and cheerful. A good sign!

"Hallo, Maddy! What's up?"

I was about to launch straight in, but just in time managed to control myself. I said, "How's James?"

I was only being polite. I'd seen him just a couple of days ago, when he'd been his usual bouncy baby self, so it wasn't as if anything was likely to have changed. But mums always enjoy telling you about their babies and sometimes I think you have to be a little bit diplomatic and not just go barging in. Mum would have been proud of me!

"So, anyway," said Jen, at last, "I don't imagine you rang just to hear about James. What can I do for you?"

"I was wondering," I said, "if you could go and have a word with Sean."

"About what, exactly?" She was already sounding guarded. But I'd given her two whole minutes of baby talk! Surely that was enough?

"About him and Danny," I said. "I thought if you could just go and talk some sense into him—"

"Talk sense into Sean? You have to be joking!"

"I'm not," I said. "I'm deadly serious. I really think someone should go and talk to him."

"Bad idea," said Jen.

"But he's unhappy! And he's your *brother*."

"He's your brother, too."

"Yes, but you're older than he is. You're his big sister! He's more likely to listen to you."

"Have you ever known Sean listen to anyone?" said Jen.

"You could at least *try*."

"And get my head bitten off? No, thank you!"

"Mine's already been bitten off," I said.

"Well, there you go! You can't run people's lives for them, Mad; specially not Sean's. Just take my advice and stay out of it cos he won't thank you for sticking your nose in. Whatever's gone wrong, it's between him and Danny. It's up to them to work it out. OK?"

No! It was not OK. I rang off, exasperated. That was Mum, Dad, Caitlyn, Jen... Was I *really* the only one who cared? The only one brave enough to actually do something?

It so wasn't fair! I'd already had my head bitten off once. But what choice did I have? Somebody had to do *something*.

I waited till Sunday morning, when I thought I was most likely to find Sean at home. I wasn't bold enough to tackle him on the telephone. I needed to be there, in person, to show him that I wasn't just interfering: I was trying to *help*. I told Mum that I was meeting Caitlyn. I don't know why I didn't simply tell her straight out that I was going to see Sean. Maybe I thought she might try to stop me. *"Oh, Maddy, I really wouldn't advise it; I really don't think you ought to!"* Why were they all such cowards?

The flat that Sean and Danny shared was in a big apartment block just a few streets away. I was confident about going there. I'd been there loads of times! I'd even been invited to the house warming when they had first moved in. It wasn't until I was actually standing outside on the pavement that the thought suddenly came to me: if they had split up, then Sean might not still be living there. I'd automatically assumed it would be Danny who'd moved out. Still, that was all right! So long as one of them was around. I could talk to Danny just as well as I could to Sean. In fact Danny might even be better. At least he wouldn't bite my head off.

I went through the main entrance and up in the lift to the second floor. I was starting to feel a bit apprehensive, almost hoping that it *was* Danny who was still there. I hated being snarled at, especially when I hadn't done anything to deserve it. But I reminded myself that it was Sean who'd stepped up and managed to convince Mum she ought to give Caitlyn an audition. We owed him big time. Both of us! Maybe I should have reminded Caitlyn how much he had done for her, though if she couldn't even find the courage to talk to Danny, she'd never in a million years be brave enough to talk to Sean. *Though I bet*, I thought, as I pressed the doorbell, *he wouldn't bite her head off.*

Just because she was Caitlyn. I was only his sister, so I didn't count.

I was about to ring the bell for a second time when the door opened. It was Sean who peered out. He was blinking, and looked half asleep.

"Oh," he said, "it's you. What d'you want?"

Not very encouraging.

"Can I come in?" I said.

"Wait." The door slammed shut. I was already beginning to wish I hadn't come. He was obviously in a foul mood.

"Right." The door opened a crack. "In! Sit." He pointed at an armchair. I obediently bounced myself down. "So. What can I do for you?"

"You look awful," I said. He was all tousled and unshaven and bleary-eyed. And still in his dressing gown. At this time of the morning!

"People tend to look awful," said Sean, "when they've only had three hours' sleep and some idiot comes clattering at the door."

"You didn't have to open it," I said. Unless maybe he'd thought it was Danny. That could be a hopeful sign! "Why have you only had three hours' sleep? Were you at a party?"

"What's this?" he said. "Some kind of interrogation? Yes! I was at a party. All right?"

"You're always at parties," I said.

A look of extreme irritation crossed his face. "And how," he said, "is that any business of yours?"

"It isn't," I said.

"Thank you! I'm glad you recognise the fact. Now, once again, what can I do for you?"

I took a breath. "Can I say something without you getting mad at me?"

"I have no idea! Why not try it and see?"

"OK!" I took another breath. "It's just... I was wondering..."

"Yes?"

"If maybe Danny doesn't like parties as much as you do!"

I knew immediately that I'd gone too far. Very coldly he said, "And you think *that* is any of your business?"

I sort of did, but I was starting to get a bit flustered. Maybe Jen had been right and I should have stayed out of it. Not that I was frightened, exactly, cos I mean it was still Sean, even if I'd never seen him that angry before. Never really seen him angry at all. Sean just doesn't *get* angry. He is usually very good-natured. I swallowed.

"You really think," he said, "that it's anything to do with you?"

I said, "No!" My voice came out as a sort of strangulated yelp. And then, to my horror, I heard it go burbling on: "I mean, *yes*, actually, if you want to know the truth! I do think it's something to do with me, cos you're my brother and Danny's like family and we all love him and I just hate it when people break up, it makes me really unhappy and I bet Danny's unhappy, too! I bet you are, as well, only you're just so pigheaded and everybody's too scared to say anything so—"

"So you thought you should be the one to come here and lecture me? Oh, get out!" He yanked open the door. "Go on. Just get out before I lose my temper!"

"Thought you already had," I muttered, as I made my way back down the stairs. I just hoped he wouldn't tell Mum or Dad. Or Jen. They'd be bound to say, "*I told you so*". Mum might even tell me off for interfering. And it wasn't even as if I'd achieved anything! Probably just made him even more pigheaded.

Slowly, dragging my feet, I wandered back home. I was almost there when my phone beeped. I pulled it out and looked at it. It was a text, from Sean.

I'm sorry I snapped at you and btw you are NOT FAT. Sean xxx

Oh! I came to a halt, in the middle of the pavement. He wasn't mad at me any more! *And btw you are NOT FAT.*

I did a little skip. Sean had apologised and I wasn't fat! If I had been, he would have told me. But he hadn't and I wasn't and tomorrow, if I wanted, I could eat chips! Caitlyn had been right all along: Danny *couldn't* have chosen me. It was nothing to do with me being fat, nothing to do with Caitlyn being better. He simply couldn't afford to be accused of favouritism. I could see that! It was all perfectly simple. Still annoying, cos I still didn't think people should be rewarded for wrong behaviour. It was shocking bad manners to pose like that in a crowded foyer! Still, maybe it was better he'd picked Caitlyn rather than someone like Tiffany. I could hardly be jealous of Caitlyn. I was her mentor! If she was doing well, it ought to make me proud and happy.

I was proud and happy. I really was! Even if she *had* behaved badly.

Chapter Eight

Suddenly it was half-term. I couldn't believe we had been at ballet school for so long. Six weeks – and they had just flown past! Livi and Jordan had rung me again to arrange a day when we could all get together.

"We so want you to meet this girl," said Livi. "The one that does the ice dancing?"

"Sonya," said Jordan. "Sonya Williams. You might have heard of her. She's very famous!"

I felt like saying, "*In ice dancing circles, maybe.*" I certainly hadn't heard of her. But then I didn't know anything about ice dancing.

"We'll ask her to come along," said Livi. "We're dying to know what you think!"

I couldn't imagine why, but I did want to see Livi and Jordan again. We had, after all, been best friends for years, and you can't just give up on old friends. Jordan said that her aunt had a restaurant in the Whittingdale Centre, and if we got there at three o'clock, after the lunchtime rush, when it was quiet, she would let us sit at one of the staff tables for as long as we liked.

"We can sit there and eat pastries," said Livi. "Well, *we* can eat pastries... dunno about you two."

"We can eat pastries," I said. I could eat anything, now Sean had told me I wasn't fat. And Caitlyn certainly wasn't.

We agreed we would meet at the entrance to the Whittingdale Centre on Tuesday afternoon. It was four stops away on the Tube, but we were quite used to travelling by ourselves. Even Caitlyn's mum, who is a rather nervous sort of person, had stopped worrying that we were going to fall over the edge of the platform or get on the wrong train and go whizzing off into the wilds of nowhere.

It was strange, seeing Livi and Jordan after so long. They looked just the same as they always had, yet somehow they seemed different. Or perhaps I was the one that was different. In the old days we would all have started babbling straight away, even if we'd just spent the whole week at school together. But now we sat awkwardly, in our deserted corner of the restaurant, with our plates of pastries, like we'd almost become strangers.

Caitlyn has always been quiet, but I am not usually short of things to say. I mean, as a rule I only have to open my mouth and it all comes bursting out. I never have to rack my brains. But today, all I could think of as a subject for conversation was life at ballet school. Incidents that had occurred in class, like Chloe getting told off for not tying her shoe ribbons properly – that is, with "ears" sticking out instead of neatly tucked away and hidden. They would just look at me, blankly. *Ears* sticking out? Ballet was a world they knew nothing about, so how could it possibly mean anything to them? Any more than their world meant very much to me, any more.

I did my best. I tried asking about people and showing an interest in what was going on, but it was like they sensed I was simply being polite.

It was Caitlyn who came to the rescue. "So where is the ice-skating person?" she said. "I thought she was going to be here?"

A stroke of genius! They immediately brightened up.

"Sonya," said Liv. "She texted us. She's going to be a bit late cos she's got a practice session that doesn't finish till two. She's always having practice sessions. She has to train five days a week! She has to be up at *six o'clock* to get there."

"You'll have loads of things in common," said Jordan. "Did Maddy tell you?" She turned eagerly to Caitlyn. "She doesn't just do skating, she actually dances! Like you do. What was that thing she was rehearsing for, the other week? Sugar Ice Fairy, or something?"

"Sugar Plum Fairy?" Caitlyn looked a bit startled. "She does that on ice?"

"I know!" shrilled Jordan. "It's incredible!"

"But how does she…" Caitlyn glanced at me, as if appealing for help. "How does she manage all the *pointe* work?"

"You mean the tippity-toe stuff? I suppose she just… goes on to the tip of her boots!"

"Wouldn't be as painful as doing it in shoes," I said.

"Maybe she just uses the music?" said Caitlyn. "And makes up her own steps? Cos I don't think you could use the *same* steps."

"Whatever she does," said Liv, "she's really good at it. She's won medals."

"Junior Championship," said Jordan.

"She's been doing it since she was five years old!"

Caitlyn said, "Maddy's been doing ballet since she was about three."

"Oh, Sonya did ballet as well, until she decided she'd rather concentrate on skating. You must admit," said Jordan, "dancing on ice is something else!"

Livi said, "Yes, I mean, dancing on a nice firm stage

must be easy compared to what she does." She giggled. "You'd probably fall flat on your face if you tried doing the Sugar Plum thingy on ice!"

Rather crushingly I said, "I wouldn't try doing the Sugar Plum thingy on ice." I tossed my head. "Sugar Plum Fairy in great big clunky boots!"

"Well, you couldn't do it, anyway," said Jordan. "Not if you're not trained for it. You'd slide about all over the place."

Jordan was making me feel rather hot and cross. I was already beginning to dislike this Sonya person.

"Actually," I said, "you're just about as wrong as could be. If you've trained for ballet, you'd have absolutely no problem skating. It's all a question of balance."

"I suppose it would be the same the other way round," mused Livi. "If you've trained as a skater you'd have no problem with b— oh!" She suddenly shot out of her seat and waved a hand at a girl who had just come into the restaurant. "Hey, Sonya!"

I'd been kind of hoping she'd be short and squat and ugly, but in fact she was quite normal-looking. Even quite prettyish if you happened to like big blue saucer eyes and dimply pink cheeks, which most everybody probably does. All the same, it was hard to imagine her dancing the Sugar Plum Fairy. She didn't really have the build for it. I didn't mean to be nasty, but it does tend to put your back up when people who were once your best friends keep telling you how amazing and wonderful and incredibly talented someone else is. Once upon a time they'd gone round telling people how it was me that was so amazing and wonderful and incredibly talented. Now it seemed they'd gone all goggle-eyed over this Sonya creature.

"Oh," she cried, very gaily, as she sat down next to Caitlyn. "Are you Maddy?"

Caitlyn said, "No, I'm Caitlyn. This is Maddy."

"Oops! My bad!" Sonya pulled a face. "But you both do ballet?"

"They're at City Ballet School," said Liv.

"You learnt ballet yourself at one time, didn't you?" urged Jordan.

"I did for a bit," agreed Sonya. "I just couldn't take the discipline. I don't know how you put up with it."

"So how many years did you do ballet?" I said.

"Only a few. I had to choose between that and skating." Sonya nibbled with little rabbity teeth round the edge of her pastry. "I could have done either. Skating just seemed more exciting. More sort of... well!" She waved a hand.

"More like a sport," I said.

"Mm... maybe. In a way."

"All those leaps and spins that you don't get in ballet."

"This is it!" cried Jordan, excitedly.

I was actually being sarcastic. Caitlyn got it: she kicked at me under the table. Sonya got it, too.

"It's just different," she said. She even sounded a bit apologetic, as if she thought she might have upset me.

"Maddy," announced Jordan, "reckons that anyone that's trained as a dancer could do ice skating."

Quickly, cos I didn't want to seem to be boasting, I explained that that wasn't actually what I'd said.

"All I meant was that if you've spent years training as a dancer you could at least manage to stay on your feet. I didn't say you could *skate*." Though to be honest I thought you probably could.

"You certainly couldn't dance," said Jordan. "Not on ice!"

"No, but she's probably right," said Sonya. "It's all to do with balance. If you wanted," she said, "you could always come along and give it a go. Both of you! If you like."

I raised an eyebrow at Caitlyn. "It might be fun," I said.

Caitlyn frowned slightly.

"*I* think it would be fun," I said.

Caitlyn said, "Y-yes... unless you went and fell over and broke something."

"She's not going to fall over," said Livi. "That's the whole point! She wants to show she can stay upright."

"And even if you did fall over," said Sonya, "you

probably wouldn't do any damage. You wouldn't actually break anything. Just a bit of a sprain, maybe. Of course, I know dancers are always terrified of injuring themselves—"

"I'm not!" I said. I had never injured myself in my life.

"So do you want to come along?"

I was very tempted – even if only to prove to Livi and Jordan that I could do it.

"You don't think she ought," said Sonya, "do you?"

She was looking at Caitlyn. Caitlyn bit her lip.

"You think it would be stupid, don't you?"

"I think it would be taking a risk," said Caitlyn.

"For goodness' sake," I cried. "I'm not made of porcelain!"

Caitlyn said, "No, but even just twisting an ankle could stop you dancing."

Caitlyn is so over cautious. I am far more of a free spirit.

"Think about it," urged Sonya. "I'll give you my number. You can always text me."

We sat in the restaurant for well over an hour, until Jordan's aunt came to tell us that they really had to close up now and start preparing for the dinner crowd. Once Sonya had joined us we seemed to have had no difficulty finding things to talk about.

"Don't forget," she said, "let me know if you want to come skating. By the way, I just remembered, there's a girl in my road that's at your ballet school... Amber something or other. Do you know her?"

I felt like saying, "*Unfortunately, yes*". But then I thought maybe she might be a friend of Sonya's and that would be rude.

"She's in our year," said Caitlyn.

"Oh," said Sonya, "small world! Is she any good?" And then, before either of us could say anything she said, "I suppose you have to be good to get in in the first place. It's one of the leading schools, isn't it? You're so lucky! I wish we had schools like that for ice skating."

"She's nice, isn't she?" said Caitlyn, as we parted company.

I agreed that she was. I couldn't help liking her even if Livi and Jordan *had* got up my nose, going on about her.

"I thought she might be all sort of... you know! Superior. Winning competitions and everything."

"She's obviously good," I said.

"At least she doesn't boast about it. But you're not *really* going to go skating with her, are you?"

"Don't see why not," I said. "Why shouldn't I?"

"*Maddy!* You might do something to yourself."

"Like what? You heard what Sonya said... you're not going to *break* anything."

"No, but you could pull a muscle or – or strain a tendon, or—"

I rolled my eyes.

"Think of the end-of-term Gala!" cried Caitlyn.

I muttered, "That's weeks away."

"Yes, but the cast lists'll be going up any time and then we'll have to start rehearsals and just imagine if you've gone and torn a ligament!"

I thought about it. I was still tempted; the end-of-term Gala wasn't all that important. Not like the big summer show, when the whole school took part and all the critics came, and the general public. This was strictly just for students and staff. It was meant as a showcase for budding choreographers in the senior school, who got to make up these really short ballets for Years Seven and Eight and choose who they wanted to dance in them. Not really a Gala at all.

"I honestly, honestly don't think you ought," said Caitlyn.

I told her that I would see how I felt.

"Life isn't any fun," I said, "if you can't try new things."

"We do try new things," said Caitlyn. "Every week!"

I said, "Yes, but it's all ballet. Just now and again you need to do something different. Otherwise," I said, "you grow stale. That's all I'm saying!"

I'd just about arrived home and was on the point of calling out to see if anyone else was around when the front door opened and Sean and Danny appeared.

"Oh," I said, "are you back together?"

"Stuck with superglue," said Sean. "Is Dad around? I need to have a word with him about the new ballet."

"Not *Narcissus*?" I said. If Dad was really going to do a ballet about Narcissus, it would be all thanks to me! "*Is* it *Narcissus*? Is he giving you a part in it?"

"Yes, and yes. Is he around?"

"I don't know," I said. "I only just got in. Did you and Danny kiss and make up?"

Sean twitched a warning eyebrow.

"I'm only asking," I said. "I'm not being nosy; I just want you to be happy."

"I am happy, thank you very much."

"Well, you weren't," I said. I turned to Danny. "He wasn't," I said. "He was all mean and miserable."

"I dispute that," said Sean.

"It's true, you were! He swore at me," I said.

"I did no such thing!"

"You almost did. You wanted to! You were mean as could be. That's why you have to kiss and make up. It's what people do when they've had a fight, otherwise it doesn't mean anything."

Sean said, "Look, just drop it, OK? You really are such a pain!"

"No, she's right," insisted Danny.

"I am," I said. "I'm right!"

"Oh, for heaven's sake," said Sean. "*There*. Are you satisfied now?"

I thought, *Not really*; it wasn't much of a kiss. But you have to know when to give up.

"Mum will be pleased," I said. "She reckons Danny's good for you. She says he's got more sense than you have."

Danny smirked. Sean said, "Charming! My own mother."

"Even *she* doesn't think you're perfect," I said. "I don't know how anyone puts up with you."

"Heartfelt agreement," said Danny.

"Look, I didn't come here to be insulted," said Sean. "I came to see Dad."

"Before you do," I said, "can I ask you something?"

"If you make it quick."

"Always in such a *hurry*," I grumbled.

"Yes, I lead a busy life. What do you want to ask me? I've already told you you're not f—"

"No, it's not that! I was just wondering, when you were a student, did you ever feel like breaking out?"

"As in breaking out of prison?"

"Yes! Well… sort of. I mean, did you ever feel a mad urge to go off and…" I waved a hand. "I don't know! Play rugby, for instance."

Sean said, "No."

"*Never?*"

"I played rugby," said Danny.

I said, "That's different! You're not a dancer. It wouldn't matter so much if you got injured. Sometimes," I said, "I just get like…" I clenched my fists. "Like there's so many things I'm not supposed to do!"

"If you feel that strongly," said Sean, "then go for it. Why not? You want to play rugby, play rugby. So you break a few bones and end your career, so what?"

I said, "I don't *want* to play rugby!"

"Well, whatever it is you're hankering after, let me just point out that once you're in the Company – assuming, of course, that you actually want to be in the Company?"

I did! Of course I did! What kind of a question was that?

"Once you're a fully paid-up member you'll find there are all sorts of exciting ways you can injure yourself... You can strain your back, you can tear a ligament, you can have muscle spasms, tendonitis, even a stress fracture if that's what takes your fancy. The choice is yours! And all that without having to resort to playing rugby, or whatever else you have in mind. Obviously something the powers-that-be wouldn't look too kindly on or you wouldn't be so desperate to get my approval."

I muttered that I wasn't desperate. "I just wanted to know if you'd ever felt that way."

"You mean, frustrated?"

"Like wanting to try something different even if people told you not to. Wouldn't you just have gone and done it anyway?"

"Absolutely not." Sean shook his head. "It's true I wasn't exactly a model student, but I can honestly say I was never tempted to do anything which might put my career in jeopardy. And if you want my opinion, I don't think you should, either."

"But all I w—"

I was about to say that all I wanted to do was go ice skating, just to prove that I could do it. I wasn't going to break my neck! Or even my leg. But Sean held up a hand.

"Don't tell me! I don't want to know. The very fact you're asking me shows you're not totally convinced. So if I were you I'd play it safe – especially with the end-of-term Gala coming up. I know everyone says, '*Oh,* it's *not that important*', but it's a great little showcase and, believe me, Madam will be out there watching like a hawk." He wagged a finger in my face. "You have been warned!"

Chapter Nine

People were *so* disappointing. Even Sean. He'd always had this reputation as being a rebel – doing his own thing, going his own way. And now here he was, telling me to *play it safe*. Sean, of all people!

I grumbled to Caitlyn about it when we met up for school the following week.

"Honestly! He's as bad as you are."

"Why?" She snatched at my words, eagerly. I might have known she would take it as a compliment, being mentioned in the same breath as Sean. "Did he tell you not to be stupid?"

"He didn't say *stupid*."

"But he did say you shouldn't do it?"

I struggled for a moment. I didn't want her gloating, just because Sean happened to agree with her.

"He just said be careful."

"But you're *not* going to do it? You're not, surely?"

"Dunno," I said. "I'm still thinking about it."

Caitlyn shook her head. "I just don't see the point."

"That's because you're not adventurous. Some of us," I said, "feel the need to push ourselves. Otherwise you just *stagnate*."

It was a good word, *stagnate*! I felt quite proud of it. At least it gave Caitlyn something to think about.

I wondered if I could persuade Chloe into coming along. *She* was always boasting about doing whatever she wanted. Not that I felt the need of company, cos after all I'd be with Sonya. I was just curious to discover if I was the only one who'd be bold enough to try something new.

I mentioned it to Chloe later that morning. At least she didn't immediately shy away in horror. She said, "Mm… it could be fun."

"So shall we go?" I said.

That was when she started to back off. "What, you mean, like, now?"

"At the weekend. There's this girl I met that does ice dancing. She's offered to take me."

"It's not a very good time," said Chloe. "I mean, they're going to start casting for the end-of-term Gala any day now."

For goodness' sake! What was wrong with people? It wasn't like I was suggesting we climb Mount Everest or go sky-diving. Just a couple of turns round an ice rink!

"Thing is," said Chloe, "I wouldn't want to do anything that might stop me getting a decent part. Like even just twisting your ankle might ruin your chances, specially if they found out how you did it. You know what they're like! If you don't dedicate every single waking hour..."

I obviously must have pulled a face, or made some noise of disgust, cos she said, "Maddy, I'm sorry, but I worked really hard to get here!"

"We all did," I said. "Don't worry about it! I can go by myself."

By now I was absolutely determined that one way or another, I was going to prove to Livi and Jordan that as a trained dancer I could put on a pair of skating boots and whizz round an ice rink without falling flat on my face. They were the ones who had doubted me, not Sonya. I was, however, beginning to think that maybe it would be wiser if I waited until the Christmas holidays. The end-of-term Gala might not be all that important, but it was still a showcase; and, as Sean had said, Madam would be out there, watching us like a hawk.

That afternoon we had Character with Mr Alessandro. The previous week we'd done the Czardas out of *Coppélia*. This week we were going to learn some of the dances from *The Three-Cornered Hat*, which is one of my favourite ballets. Caitlyn caught my eye and gave me a big grin. She knew all about my passion for everything Spanish!

It was Roz who poked me in the ribs and hissed, "Have you seen?"

I hissed back at her: "Seen what?"

"Over there." She jerked her head towards the corner of the room. I swivelled round to take a look. A girl was sitting there. I recognised her as someone from Year Nine. Carey something or other. Carey Ellison! I could guess why she was there. She had obviously been given permission to come and check us out and choose who she wanted to use in her end-of-term showpiece. Presumably something which featured character work.

Character was one of my strengths! I'd only really discovered this since being at CBS cos we'd hardly touched on it with Mum. I think secretly Mum considers character dancing a bit inferior to strictly classical, though I could be wronging her. It might just be she didn't have time for it in the syllabus. When Sean had made his debut in *El Amor Brujo* she said it was one of the best things he'd ever done. But then that was Spanish. Nobody could say Spanish was inferior!

As we filed out at the end of class, Carey came over
to me.

"You're very good at this," she said. "You obviously
enjoy it."

I beamed rather foolishly and said, "I do!"

"Mm." She nodded. "Excellent!"

Roz and Caitlyn couldn't wait to come scuttling up
to me.

"What did she want?" breathed Roz. "What did she say?"

"Oh… just said I obviously enjoyed doing Character."

"Wow! You know what that means, don't you?"

I thought I probably did, but I certainly wasn't going
to admit to it. Too much like tempting fate! Caitlyn,
obligingly, said it for me.

"It means she's got you earmarked… so it's just as
well you didn't do you-know-what!"

"What, what?" squealed Roz. "What didn't she do?"

"Maddy knows," said Caitlyn.

Three days later, the cast lists went up. At the top
was a piece called *Winter Dreams:*

WINTER DREAMS by Jocelyn Wang
The Spirit of Winter .... Caitlyn Hughes

"Omigod!" cried Alex. "You've got a whole piece to yourself!"

Caitlyn, as usual, was modest about it. "It's probably nothing much," she said; but her cheeks had fired up and I could tell she was thrilled. Who wouldn't be?

There were five other pieces with small casts of just three or four people; and then there was Carey's piece.

BALLET OF THE DOLLS by Carey Ellison

I ran my eye quickly down the cast list, searching for my name. *French Doll, Rag Doll, Russian Dolls, Spanish D—*

Miki Karashima? I felt my heart squeeze itself into a tight ball of shock. Miki Karashima as the Spanish Doll?

"Woohoo!" cried Chloe. "I'm a Skittle! Hey, Roz, you're a Russian Doll! So's Amber. Mei, you're a *Chinese* Doll!"

"China Doll, actually," said Tiffany.

"What's the difference?"

"China Doll doesn't come from China. It's *made* of china."

"Oh! That figures. Mei could be made of china… all tiny and fragile. What's she cast you as?"

"French Doll." Tiffany said it rather smugly. Probably waiting for someone to say how *chic* and Frenchified she was.

"What about Maddy? What's she down as?"

"*Clown?*" Roz sounded like she thought it must be some mistake. "She wants you to dance a *Clown?* So who's d—" She broke off. "*Miki Karashima?* That's crazy! How could she choose her instead of you?" Roz swung round, indignantly. "After what she said to you!"

I swallowed. There is such a thing as pride.

"Obviously she thinks she's more suited to the part."

"But everyone knows you're brilliant at the Spanish stuff."

"Well…" I shrugged. "Maybe she is, too." She was in

Year Eight so I'd never actually seen her dance. But she couldn't be better than I was! I just didn't believe it. Not after Carey had gone out of her way to tell me I was excellent.

I forced myself to go back to the cast list. I wasn't even a Spinning Top! Even though spinning was one of my strong points. Nico was an Action Man. Oliver and Carlo were Acrobats. I wouldn't have minded so much being an Acrobat. Maybe even a Juggler. But all I was, was a Clown. Not even *the* Clown: *a* Clown. There was a whole bunch of us! Four in all.

"Roz is right," said Caitlyn, later. "It doesn't make any sense! Even Mr Alessandro said your Spanish dancing was *muy auténtico*."

"I knew I should have gone skating," I said. "I might just as well have done, mightn't I? For all the difference it makes."

Very earnestly Caitlyn said that while she still thought it was stupid, not casting me as the Spanish Doll, it wasn't necessarily a bad thing being cast as a Clown.

"Clowns are fun! She probably chose you because she knows you're good at making people laugh."

I thought, *Yes*, but that still didn't change anything. I was still just one of four. It was all very well for Caitlyn, *she* was a soloist. *The Spirit of Winter*... alone in the spotlight. I felt like I'd been relegated to the corps de ballet.

Mum asked me that evening whether the cast lists had gone up yet.

I said, "Which cast lists?" Like I didn't know.

"Which ones do you think?" said Mum. "For the Gala!"

"Oh," I said. "Those. No, we're still waiting."

I'm not usually a coward, but how could I tell Mum that Caitlyn was dancing *The Spirit of Winter* and I was just a boring Clown? She might not actually *say* anything; she wouldn't have to. She would simply pinch her lips into a thin line and give me one of her looks. Long, and hard, and withering. Even Sean had been known to wilt under one of Mum's looks. She was the only person I knew who could reduce him to silence. And if she could do that to Sean, what chance did I stand? I would tell her later, cos obviously I would have to. But right at this moment I couldn't face it.

The following week the rehearsal schedules went up. I was relieved that to begin with, at any rate, Carey was taking us all separately rather than calling the whole cast. I'd been dreading the prospect of having to watch Miki learning what I thought of as my part. It *should* have been my part! Everyone thought so. I had this strange feeling that even Carey thought so. She greeted me quite awkwardly when I turned up for the first rehearsal.

"Oh, Maddy," she said. And then there was a bit of a pause, and I thought she was going to say something else, but at that moment the others came in and rather lamely she said, "Good! We're all here. Let's get started."

The other three, a girl called Veena and two boys, Marek and Tom, were all Year Eights. I knew them, of course, but had no idea what sort of dancers they were. They seemed quite happy to have been cast as Clowns.

Tom admitted that it would have been nicer to be a soloist, but, "All the solo parts have gone to girls."

That hadn't struck me before. I told him that that was extremely sexist, but Tom didn't seem too bothered. He just shrugged his shoulders and said, "I guess dolls are usually female."

"Not always," I said. "What about Batman? She could have had a Batman doll. Or a sailor doll, or a spaceman doll, or a – a football doll, or a – well! Almost anything."

Tom agreed, though not with any particular sense of outrage. "She could have, I suppose. But they're not really what you'd call traditional, are they?"

So who wanted to be traditional? This was the twenty-first century! The more I thought about it, the more I thought that he and Marek had been let down just as badly as I had.

"I mean, really," I said, "*clowns*. They're so dated!"

"Oh, I dunno," said Tom. "They're still around."

"But what do they *do*? Apart from look stupid."

"Well, I guess they make people laugh?"

"Never made me laugh," I said.

"Did me," said Tom. "I used to love 'em!"

That was the point at which I gave up. Tom obviously had no ambition whatsoever. Marek, sounding sympathetic, told me that, "You just have to make best… find something good."

I didn't like it, but I knew that Marek was right. And I knew that Mum would agree with him. There could be absolutely no excuse for *not* finding something good, no matter what the part. No matter how small or how insignificant. *You just have to make best…*

I tried to make best. I really did! But somewhere inside me there was this simmering well of resentment.

Carey clapped her hands and cried, "Please, guys! Remember these are clowns… they're meant to be fun!"

But I'd never thought that clowns were fun. I'd never really liked them, even when I was tiny. Great stupid things clumping round in their outsize boots and their big baggy costumes. I'd never seen the point of them.

"Cheer up," said Tom. "It could have been worse...
She could have picked you as Baby Doll."

I said, "There isn't any Baby Doll!"

"Barbie Doll?"

I snapped that there wasn't one of those, either. I don't know why I was snapping at Tom. He was a nice boy and he was only trying to help. It wasn't his fault Carey had gone and got my hopes up only to cruelly dash them and stamp them underfoot. She was the one I should be snapping at, not Tom. I still had this feeling there was something she wanted to say to me. Like sorry, maybe? She'd been so friendly before. Now she was hardly saying a word, hardly even looking at me, except when she had to cos I wasn't doing her stupid steps the way she wanted. Stupid *clown* steps. Stupid music, stupid make-up, stupid costumes. Tom could say what he liked, I refused to be comforted.

As we left the studio we passed Miki, on her way in. She gave us this radiant smile.

"This is so fun!" she said. And then she snapped her fingers and went "*Olé!*"

I tried not to glower at her. She wasn't to know she'd been given the part that I should have had and that I was simmering with resentment. *But really*, I thought, *it was too ridiculous!* Miki was absolutely tiny, like some kind of miniature porcelain ornament. She couldn't have been more wrong for a Spanish Doll!

I simmered all the rest of the day. I was still simmering when my phone buzzed as I was on my way home with Caitlyn. It was a text from Sonya.

So! Wanna come skating? This wkend?

I showed it to Caitlyn.

"Oh, Maddy," she wailed, "you're not going to?"

I said, "Why not?"

What was there to stop me? Even if I did fall over and break something, not that I intended to, but what if I did? Who wanted to dance a stupid Clown anyway? Some showcase that was likely to be!

 169

Defiantly, as Caitlyn watched, I texted back: *Yes! What time, where?*

I turned to Caitlyn. "Don't you dare start lecturing me!"

"Wasn't going to," said Caitlyn.

I said, "Good, well, don't!"

People that were lucky enough to be given solo roles, not to mention getting themselves included in books of photographs, would do best, in my opinion, to just KEEP QUIET.

I arranged to see Sonya at her ice rink on Saturday afternoon.

"It's going to be a bit crowded," she said, as we met up, "cos it's general public. You're not allowed to go mad and start racing round at top speed, but you shouldn't anyway, as it's your first time. And I won't be able to show you any of my routines, I'm afraid. There'll be far too many people."

I said that was all right, I knew the sort of thing she did.

"I went on YouTube and found some videos... I even found one of somebody doing the Sugar Plum Fairy."

Eagerly she said, "What did you think?"

I said, "Well…" I really liked Sonya. She wasn't at all boastful about her achievements and I didn't want to sound superior, like Mum, but it hadn't seemed to me that a Sugar Plum Fairy on ice really had very much going for it.

"You didn't like it, did you?" said Sonya.

"It wasn't that I didn't like it," I said. "I can see that you'd have to be incredibly good at skating to be able to do it, but… I think maybe I'm too used to seeing the real thing. I mean, you know… the actual dance. On stage. In *Nutcracker*."

"That's all right," said Sonya. "Nobody ever said ice dancing's the same as ballet. Liv and Jordan are going to join us, by the way. I said we'll see them inside. Is that OK? They're not going to skate; they just want to watch."

"Just want to see if I fall over," I said.

"I'm sure you won't," said Sonya. "You're like all dancers… lots of poise."

Poise. I liked that! I was beginning to warm to Sonya more and more. I didn't even mind when she started mothering me, sternly informing me that I was to stay by her side – "Not go taking off on your own" – and not even *attempt* anything advanced, like spinning or jumping.

"Today it's just the basics," she said. "And, here, I brought this along for you."

I said, "Foot powder?"

"Yes! I don't need it," said Sonya, "cos I've got my own boots. But you'll have to hire some and even though they spray them you can't afford to take chances. Not as a dancer."

I thought, *This is like being out with my mum!*

"See, I feel responsible for you," said Sonya. "I don't want you getting athlete's foot and then blaming me."

I promised that I wouldn't dream of blaming her. "I was the one that decided to come. You didn't make me. And anyhow, nothing's going to happen!"

Nothing would have done had it not been for some great clumsy boy sending me flying. I'd been doing so well! Not so much as a wobble. Sonya said, "You're a natural. I thought you would be."

I asked her if I could just try one little jump, but she was very firm.

"Not this time. Maybe if you come again."

"Well, at least," I begged, "can I just go round once more? On my own?"

She said, "All right. But no racing!"

I wasn't the one who was racing; it was the great clumsy boy. As he zipped past me, doing about a hundred miles per hour, he suddenly lost his balance, crashed into me, and brought us both down hard on the ice. I heard two little shrieks from Livi and Jordan, who'd been watching my progress and crying, "Way to go!" every time I passed them.

"Maddy!" Sonya came skating over, full of concern. "Are you all right?"

I said, "No problem!" I was a dancer: dancers know how to fall.

"That was *such* bad manners," said Sonya, as the boy

picked himself up. "*And* it's against the rules. I could report you for that!"

The boy, bright red, mumbled a guilty apology. I almost felt sorry for him. In spite of looking so angelic, with her big baby eyes and her little dimpled cheeks, Sonya could obviously be quite scary.

"Good," she said, watching as the boy went limping off. "He's hurt himself. Serves him right! You're not supposed to go that fast when the rink's full of people. Are you sure you're OK?"

"I'm fine," I said. I hate being fussed over.

"I'd feel really guilty," said Sonya, "if you'd injured yourself."

"I haven't," I said. "Look – see?" I did a little daring twirl. "Perfectly all right!"

My wrist was a bit sore, but a wrist is nothing. Not like a foot, or an ankle.

"Well, anyway," said Sonya, "you've proved you could do it." She turned and waved at Livi and Jordan. "I told them you would!"

Chapter Ten

Next morning when I woke up I found that my wrist was all swollen. It was also bright purple, and painful. It made me yelp when I just waggled my fingers. I probed it cautiously. It didn't feel broken. Not that I really knew how it would feel if it had been, but there weren't any odd lumps or bumps or bones sticking out, so I thought that almost certainly it was just a sprain, or even just a bruise. Nothing to get fussed about. All I had to do was not use it for a bit and the swelling would soon go down.

I certainly wasn't going to tell Mum about it. She would immediately want to know how I'd done it, and just saying I'd tripped over wasn't likely to satisfy her.

Dancers aren't supposed to trip over! Fortunately it was the winter term, which meant long sleeves, so I could easily hide it from her and Dad. Where I couldn't hide it was at school, and especially not in dance classes. Even long-sleeved leotards don't completely cover your wrists. It was Mei, as we changed for our first session, who shrieked, "Maddy, what have you done?"

Everyone instantly spun round to see.

"It's only a bruise," I said.

Amber pulled a face. "Yuck! It's all colours of the rainbow."

I held it out, admiringly. "Pretty, isn't it?"

"You wait till Miss Eldon sees it!" said Tiffany. "*She* won't think it's very pretty. Imagine dancing *Sylphides* looking like something out of a horror movie!"

"I'm not going to be dancing *Sylphides*," I said.

"Probably won't be dancing anything at all," said Amber.

"Course I will!" I dismissed the notion, scornfully. "It's not as if it's broken or anything."

"But how did it happen?" Alex wanted to know.

I hesitated. I hadn't yet had time to decide what I was going to tell people. Caitlyn was looking at me reproachfully. "Maddy," she hissed, "you didn't?"

It was hardly more than a whisper. But Tiffany, with her great flapping ears, was on it in a flash.

"Didn't what?"

"Fall over?" said Caitlyn.

"Ooh," squealed Amber, "is that what you did?"

Looking very hard at Caitlyn I said, "Read my lips: I DID NOT FALL OVER."

Tiffany, wildly excited, shrieked, "So how did you do it?"

"Somebody crashed into me," I said. I looked rather hard at Caitlyn as I said it, but she just shook her head.

"You should sue them," said Tiffany. "Look at the state of you!"

"It'll clear up," I said. "It's nothing serious."

Miss Eldon, needless to say, homed in on it immediately.

"Maddy," she said, "what on earth have you done to yourself?"

I told her that someone had pushed me and made me fall over. "It isn't anything. It's just a bit sore."

"Well, it looks very nasty. Have you been to the nurse?"

"It's only a bruise," I said. "Honestly!"

"Nevertheless, I'd like you to go and get it checked. Please do it as soon as you can. All right?"

As soon as class was over I dutifully took myself off to the nurse's office, only to be told what I'd known all along: it was just a bruise.

"I'm afraid it's going to be a bit sore for a while, but try rubbing some arnica in it. That should help."

"I don't even need it strapped up," I told Caitlyn, triumphantly, later in the day. "It's all a great fuss about nothing!"

"But how did it happen?" said Caitlyn. "If you didn't fall over—"

"I told you," I said. "It was just one of those things.

There was this stupid boy, going round far too fast. He went and crashed straight into me! Sonya was absolutely furious; she threatened to report him. But at least I proved I could do it! Livi and Jordan were there. *I* think they were secretly hoping I'd fall over, but I didn't. Honestly, it's easy as pie! Sonya thinks I'm a natural. She thinks if I took it up seriously I could go in for competitions, like she does. I might even reach Olympic standard!"

"She said that?" said Caitlyn.

Well, she hadn't *quite* said that; but she'd certainly been impressed.

"So are you going to?"

"What? Take it up seriously?" I gave a little twirl. "Who knows? I might try going again with Sonya. Maybe some time when it's not so crowded, so I could try a few jumps and spins."

Caitlyn didn't say anything, just pursed her lips.

"*Now* what?" I said. "Honestly! You look like you've sucked on a lemon!"

"I can't help it," said Caitlyn. "I just think it was really irresponsible of you."

I blinked. "Oh," I said. "Well! Thank you very much. Some support *that* is."

"I'm sorry," she said, "but sometimes it seems like you've just had everything too easy. You've never had to fight for it like the rest of us. Being a dancer, being at ballet school... you just take it for granted. It doesn't mean that much to you."

Such cheek! How did she know how much it meant to me?

"It means every bit as much," I said.

"That's what you *say*," said Caitlyn. "But if it really meant as much to you as it does to me you wouldn't be prepared to run the risk of messing it all up."

Messing it all up? What on earth was she on about? All I'd wanted to do was try something different!

"I just wanted to prove that I could do it," I said.

"You mean you just wanted to show Livi and Jordan that you were as good as Sonya."

"Oh, please!" I said. Why should I care about Livi and Jordan? What did they know about skating? Nothing! Any more than they knew about ballet.

"It's true," insisted Caitlyn. "You should have seen your face when they kept going on about Sonya and how brilliant she was."

"Should have seen yours!" I retorted. I remembered the looks we'd exchanged. It wasn't only me.

"Actually," said Caitlyn, "I thought it was quite funny, to tell you the truth. You were getting all steamed up and they had no idea; they just went babbling on."

"Ha ha, it must have been very amusing," I said.

"Well, it was for me," agreed Caitlyn. "But then I wasn't the one they were always boasting about. Always telling everybody how they were friends with you, and how your mum and dad were famous, and your brother was Sean O'Brien, and—"

"Oh," I cried, "I never realised you were so jealous!"

I didn't give her a chance to reply, just turned and stalked off. It was the nearest we had ever come to a quarrel. It didn't help that deep down I suspected Caitlyn could be right. It wasn't so much that I'd wanted to try something new as that I'd resented the way Livi and Jordan had switched their loyalty from me to Sonya. But that didn't mean she had to turn on me the way she had! Unless all this time *she'd* been resenting *me*? Except why should she? I'd never boasted about my family! And if it hadn't been for them – well, Mum and Sean – *and* me – she would never have had ballet lessons in the first place. How could she be so mean? After all I'd done to help her?

I was still seething when I turned up for another boring clown rehearsal only to have Carey come storming over to me in some kind of demented rage. I stared at her in astonishment. What was *her* problem?

"Madeleine O'Brien," she said, "I am absolutely livid with you!"

I said, "Why?" What was I supposed to have done?

"Did you know that Miki Karashima's gone down with

glandular fever and won't be well enough to come back until next term?"

Bemused, I shook my head.

"I've just asked Miss Hickman if *now* she'll let me have you for the part of the Spanish Doll and guess what?" She was practically spitting, she was so angry. "She still says I can't!"

"If it's because of my wrist," I said, "it's only a bruise! It'll be gone in a day or two."

"Try telling that to Miss Hickman. She seems to think I'll be lucky if I can keep you as a Clown."

"But it's just a bruise!" I cried. I desperately hadn't wanted to be a Clown, but I had to be *something*. I couldn't *not* have a part in the end-of-term Gala!

"What shall I do?" I stared rather wildly at Carey. "Should I go and talk to her?"

"Be my guest," said Carey. "Just don't blame me if she freezes you out. She's in a really foul mood! You've obviously done something to upset her."

I said, "I haven't done anything!"

★ 183 ☆

"Well, OK, give it a go and see what happens. I'll say one thing," said Carey, "you might be a pain, but you've got a lot of guts. Just as well," she added, "cos you're certainly going to need them!" She turned and clapped her hands. "Right, you guys! Let's get started. And just remember, it's meant to be *funny*."

I was pleased Carey thought I had guts, but truth to tell even I shrank from the prospect of tackling Miss Hickman in a foul mood. She was never very jolly at the best of times. Certainly not warm and smiley like Miss Eldon, or generous like Mr Alessandro. She could actually be quite mean. Plus I had a sneaking feeling that for some reason she didn't particularly like me. But I couldn't just sit back and say nothing! If I'd done something to make her mad at me, I needed to know what it was. What was I supposed to be guilty of? And what had Carey meant when she said she'd asked Miss Hickman if she could *now* have me for the part of the Spanish Doll? Did that mean I was the one she'd wanted from the start? And if so, why hadn't Miss Hickman let her? And why had she told Carey that she *still* couldn't have me?

It was the end of the day before I finally nerved myself to go along to the Office and beg Miss Preedy for an appointment. Miss Preedy is Miss Hickman's secretary. She is very protective, and guards Miss Hickman as if she is some kind of god.

"Ah, Madeleine," she said, peering at me over the top of her spectacles. "There you are."

She didn't say it in what could be called an encouraging sort of way. Not like, *Ah, Madeleine, how lovely to see you!* More like, *Ah, Madeleine. YOU.*

Not very comforting.

She slid her spectacles further down her nose and peered at me a bit more. It was like I was some kind of object that had dragged itself out of the slime.

"What can I do for you?"

"Please would it be possible," I said, "to see Miss Hickman?"

I expected her to snap at me that it most certainly

wouldn't! Miss Hickman was busy, or was in a meeting, or had gone home, and I would have to come back tomorrow. Instead, rather disturbingly, she said that it would be perfectly possible.

"Miss Hickman wanted to see you, anyway. Let me just check." She pressed a button on her phone. "I have Madeleine O'Brien here. Would you like me to send her in?"

I listened, with a growing sense of foreboding. What did Miss Hickman want to see *me* for? It was supposed to be me wanting to see her!

"All right, Madeleine." Miss Preedy waved a hand towards Miss Hickman's door. "She'll see you now. You can go in."

Just for a moment I had a little burst of hope. Maybe Miss Hickman was going to tell me that alone out of my year I'd been chosen to take part in the Company's Christmas production of *Nutcracker*. Maybe that was why Carey had said she'd be lucky to even just have me as a Clown? No wonder she was so cross! A lowly first year dancing with the Company? Messing up her end-of-term production piece?

It was a beautiful idea, but I think I knew in my heart it was only make-believe. I told myself that I had a lot of guts. Carey had said so! And why anticipate the worst? It might never happen – or so Dad was always telling us. Of course, as Mum was invariably quick to add, if by any chance it *did*, you just had to be brave and face up to it.

I was brave! At least, I'd always thought I was. Suddenly I wasn't so sure.

I swallowed a lump in my throat and tapped at the door. Miss Hickman's voice, light and sharp, called, "Come!"

I hesitated. Across the room, Miss Preedy nodded impatiently and made shooing motions with her hands.

"Off you go!"

With an ominous sinking feeling I opened the door – and knew at once that the worst had arrived. My beautiful idea had indeed been make-believe. Whatever

Miss Hickman wanted to see me for, it wasn't to tell me I'd been chosen to dance with the Company.

"Well, now, Maddy."

She gave me a frosty smile. Except that it wasn't really a smile, more like a slight stretching of the lips. She sat there, straight-backed, cold as a statue, behind her desk. Acres and acres of it, stretching emptily between us. Nothing on it but a telephone, a laptop and a neat pile of folders. Not even a photograph, to show she was human.

"Sit down, please."

There were three chairs in the room. Two were plump and comfortable, one was hard and uninviting. The one she waved me to was the hard and uninviting one. I perched myself uneasily on the extreme edge – and immediately started to slide off. Miss Hickman watched, without saying anything, as I wriggled myself back on.

"If you're finally settled? Good! Then let us proceed. I wanted to see you, Maddy. I've been thinking for a while now that we should have a talk. This incident with your wrist…"

I tugged, unobtrusively, at the sleeve of my sweatshirt, trying to pull it down over my hand, but too late. Miss Hickman's eyes, like chips of ice, had already homed in on it, shooting frost daggers across the desk.

"I understand that against all advice you insisted on going ice skating and that that is how you injured yourself."

I felt my cheeks fire up. Who had told Miss Hickman that I had been ice skating? Nobody knew! A small voice inside me whispered, *Caitlyn knew…* I pushed the thought to the back of my mind. Caitlyn wouldn't tell on me!

"Is this true?" said Miss Hickman.

I said, "Y-yes, but—"

"No buts, Maddy! I don't wish to hear any buts. You were advised not to go, and you insisted on doing so. And at this point in the term! With the Gala coming up. You obviously gave no thought whatsoever to any inconvenience you might cause, especially to poor Carey. I am in two minds whether to let you appear in the Gala at all. I may very well tell her that she will have to find someone else – or make do with one dancer less. I have not yet decided, but I have to warn you that I am strongly tempted. It will be hard on her; I've already had to disappoint her once. She originally wanted you for the more showy part of the Spanish Doll – for which, of course, you are very well suited. You might find it instructive to know why, that being the case, I vetoed the suggestion. Frankly," said Miss Hickman, "it was nothing to do with your ability, but rather your commitment. You have yet to convince me how much it actually means to you, becoming a dancer. I wonder, Maddy—"

Miss Hickman leaned forward, elbows on the desk, and made a steeple of her hands. She gazed at me sternly over the top of them.

"I wonder if you have ever asked yourself why it was that we hesitated to take you in the first place?

Possibly you never realised that we hesitated. But we did! You were one of our borderline cases. Had it not been for another student opting at the last moment to go elsewhere –" Miss Hickman's lip curled as she said the word *elsewhere* – "the probability is that you would not have been offered a place. It seemed to some of us then, as it seems to me now, that your attitude towards your studies is somewhat… how shall I put it? Lacking."

I sat in stunned silence. I couldn't have spoken even if she'd expected me to, which quite obviously she didn't.

"Here at City Ballet we ask a great deal of our students," said Miss Hickman. "We expect total dedication. Nothing less, Maddy, will satisfy us. We can always tell, you know, what a student is thinking. We can spot the one who values outside interests more than the ballet. The one who starts questioning whether it's really worth it. It all comes out in their work. Technique can cover a multitude of sins; what it cannot do is disguise the basic attitude. Do you have anything to say in your defence?"

I clutched with both hands at the seat of my chair. "I'm-very-sorry-I-went-skating-I-just-wanted-to-see-if-I-could-do-it!"

The words shot out of me. Miss Hickman's eyebrows rose, incredulously, into her hairline.

"You never stopped to think what would happen if you injured yourself? You never gave so much as a second's thought to Carey and her ballet. Did you?"

Dumbly I shook my head.

"She's devoted so much of her time and energy to this project, it means so much to her, and now – well! As I say, I am still considering my options. I am even forced to consider whether you are in fact suitable material for CBS at all. I should be loath to ask your parents to remove you, especially given their close ties to the Company, but unless I see a marked improvement over the coming term I may well feel I have no choice. For the moment my main concern is the Gala and whether you should be allowed to take part. I have to tell you that my inclination is strongly against it. I shall ponder the question and let you know. Now…" She waved a hand, dismissing me. "Go!"

Chapter Eleven

As I left Miss Hickman's room, my eyes fixed firmly on the outer door, Miss Preedy called after me. "All right?"

She sounded concerned, like maybe she knew what Miss Hickman had been going to say and was feeling sorry for me. Miss Preedy! Actually feeling *sorry*.

I didn't trust my voice enough to attempt anything in reply. I just made a vague mumbling sound, wrenched open the door and fled.

It was the end of the day and most people, thank goodness, had already gone home. The last thing I wanted was to bump into someone like Tiffany. I was just glad I'd told Caitlyn not to bother waiting for me cos I honestly didn't know what I would say to her. If

I asked her straight out whether it was her who'd told Miss Hickman about the ice skating, would she admit it? And if I asked her why she'd done it, would she tell me? She could hardly try claiming it wasn't her, because who else could it have been? There wasn't anybody else who knew, other than Sonya. Well, and Livi and Jordan. But why would any of them want to tell on me? And how could they have done, anyway? They didn't even know Miss Hickman.

I stumbled my way down the stairs towards the main exit. A small group of Company members were also heading there. Sean was among them, but I didn't call out to him as I normally would. Instead I shrank back into the shadows, waiting for them to go past. I desperately didn't want to be seen! But then at the last moment, as he was about to follow the others through the door, Sean happened to glance over his shoulder.

"Mads?" he said. "Is that you?" He closed the door and turned back up the corridor. "Are you OK?"

I gave this big bright smile and said, "Yes, I'm fine!"

Unfortunately I felt my eyes filling with tears even as I said it.

"Hey!" Sean put an arm round me and gave me a hug. "What's wrong?"

I said, "Everything!"

"Oh, now, come on, chin up," said Sean. "It can't be as bad as all that!"

"It's worse," I sobbed. The tears by now were spilling over and making waterfalls down my cheeks. I tilted my head back, trying to stop them. "It's the end of everything!"

"Want to tell me about it?"

"I can't!" I shook my head vigorously, spraying tears everywhere. "Not here."

A couple of senior students were coming along the corridor. They glanced at me curiously as they passed.

"OK," said Sean, "I'll tell you what... I'm not on tonight so how about I take you home with me, give you a cup of tea and you pour out all your troubles. How's that?"

I sniffed, and wiped the back of my hand across my nose. "I don't like tea!"

"So whaddya want? Whisky?"

Startled, I said, "Really?"

"No, not really! You can make do with what you're given."

"Mango juice?" I said. "I love mango juice!"

"Whatever we happen to have in the fridge! Don't be so picky. You either want to get things off your chest or—"

"I do," I said, "I do!"

"So come on, then, let's go."

"Will Danny be there?" I said, as we walked to the Underground.

"Probably not, I think he's working. Why? Did you want him to be?"

I said, "No! Just you."

He squeezed my hand. "Don't worry, we'll get things sorted."

"You can't," I said. "Nobody can!"

★ 197 ☆

"Don't be such a drama queen," said Sean. "Let's just wait and see."

Once at the flat, Sean sat me down on the sofa with a glass of lemonade – "Sorry, no mango juice, but at least this has bubbles," – and pulled up a chair.

"Right! Tell me what's happened."

I took a deep, trembly breath. "It's Miss Hickman," I said.

"What about her?"

"She hates me!"

"She hates a lot of people," said Sean.

"But she hates me specially!"

"So tell me about it! I'm here, I'm listening… what's she done? I can't help you, Mads, if you won't tell me what's upset you. Dry your eyes, blow your nose, have a sip of lemonade – and off you go!"

Once I got started, the words just came tumbling out. How Carey had wanted me for the part of the Spanish Doll, but Miss Hickman had said she couldn't cos she didn't think I was committed enough, and now she was saying that maybe she wouldn't let me be in the Gala at all and she might even ask me to leave if my attitude didn't change, and all I'd done was just go ice skating, and if Caitlyn hadn't told her she wouldn't even have known and it wasn't like I'd broken anything, it was only a bruise, and if she'd let me dance the Spanish Doll like Carey had wanted I wouldn't have gone skating in the first place, I only went cos I was really upset, cos I *should* have been the Spanish Doll, everybody said so, even Miss Hickman said I was right for it, and now the girl that had been going to dance it instead of me was off sick and she *still* wouldn't let me have the part. "She's not even thinking about what's best for Carey's ballet! She just wants to punish *me*."

Sean listened, gravely, as I poured out the story. Unlike Mum and Dad, he is a very easy person to confide in. It's true that for most of the time we have this kind of jokey relationship, where he teases me and I respond with what he calls smart mouth, but I always know that he'll be there for me if I need him.

"It seems to me," he said, at last, "that Liz Hickman's definitely got it in for you. You've obviously rubbed her up the wrong way – which is a very easy thing to do. I've done it myself, on several occasions. The woman has no sense of humour whatever. On the other hand, of course, she does have right on her side: it *was* pretty stupid to go skating this near the Gala. I can understand why you did it, and I'm sure she can, too. Anyone else might have given you a bit of a talking to and left it at that. She's obviously bent on teaching you a lesson. The thing you have to understand about Liz Hickman is that if she can break a person, she will. There are those like Caitlyn, who don't need to be broken; she'll happily toe the line. Then there are others, like you, who'll fight her all the way. She doesn't care for that. But if you can come through it—"

"Like you did."

"It was easier for me. We had our spats, but she treats men differently. We're still at a bit of a premium."

"What's—" I hiccupped. "What's that mean?"

"It means that even today there are probably a thousand little girls desperate to do ballet for every ten boys. She couldn't afford to be too high-handed. But one thing I do think you have to ask yourself is whether there's any possibility she's right... *Are* you totally committed?"

"I am," I said, "I am! I don't know why everyone thinks I'm not."

"Who thinks you're not? Apart from Liz Hickman."

"Mum does! Well, she used to. It's why she wouldn't let me go full-time until I was thirteen, cos she didn't think I had enough discipline. And Caitlyn! She thinks I've had it too easy. She said that's why it doesn't mean as much to me as it does to her."

"I guess in one sense," said Sean, "that could be true. You've always grown up with the knowledge that you'll become a dancer. For her it was just a dream."

"But I was the one who helped her! If it hadn't been for me—"

"It would still be just a dream. I hear you."

"So how could she be so horrible? Even if she *was* jealous!"

"You think she was jealous?"

"Why else would she have done it?"

Sean frowned. "Are you absolutely certain it was Caitlyn?"

"She's the only one it could be!"

Sean was silent a moment. "Have you actually asked her about it?"

"No! I don't want to talk to her."

"Hmm." He gazed at me, thoughtfully. "What is Caitlyn doing for the Gala?"

The tears came welling back up. "She's got a s-solo."

"So she really has no reason to be jealous? It sounds as if she's doing quite well."

"Thanks to me!"

"It's true you might have been the one who got her started, but let's face it, since then she's made her own way. Be fair!"

I didn't want to be fair. *She* hadn't been; why should

I? I found a bit of crumpled tissue in my pocket and tugged it out. It immediately tore in half, which set me sobbing all over again.

"What am I going to say to Mum?"

"Can I make a suggestion?" said Sean. "If I were you, I wouldn't say anything to Mum. Not at this moment. Give it twenty-four hours. The woman might have a change of heart."

"She hasn't got a heart!"

"What passes for a heart. Alternatively she might just simmer down and have a rethink. It doesn't really make much sense to stop you dancing. It's not just punishing you, but punishing whatever her name is – Carey? It's punishing her, as well. That's hardly very fair. I wonder if I should go and have a word with her?"

"With Miss Hickman?"

"Well, or I could take it directly to Madam if you like. She's a bit of a tartar, but she'll listen to reason. What do you think? Shall I give it a go?"

I so wanted to say yes. "Yes, yes! *Give it a go!*" Sean

was one of Madam's favourites. If anyone could get round her, he could. And Madam's word was law. Miss Hickman might be Head of Dance, but it was Madam who ran the Company. On the other hand…

"You're looking doubtful," said Sean. "Do you not want me to?"

I did! I so did! But wouldn't it be the very thing Tiffany had accused me of? Using my family to get special treatment?

"Look, I'm happy to do it," said Sean. "I'm not saying you haven't been a bit irresponsible and I don't doubt you deserved a good talking to, but this is way over the top. Let me go and speak to Madam."

I struggled for a moment. If you've got connections, why not use them? That was what I'd always felt. But if Sean spoke to Madam and Madam spoke to Miss Hickman, might that not make Miss Hickman hate me even more?

I was still struggling when we heard the sound of the front door being opened.

"That'll be Danny," said Sean.

I caught at his arm. "Don't say anything!"

"You mean to Danny or to Madam?"

"Maybe both?" I said.

"Fair enough, if that's what you want. I'll be silent as the grave! Now, let's get you home, and in the meantime, just hang loose, don't mention anything to Mum, and we'll see what happens. OK?"

"OK." I blotted again at my eyes. I was glad we were going to keep things secret, though I couldn't help wondering whether Sean would say anything to Danny when they were alone together. I thought he probably would cos when people are couples they always seem to tell each other everything. Up until today I'd always told Caitlyn everything. Not any more! I wasn't sure I could even bear to speak to her again.

I managed to spend most of next morning not speaking. To Caitlyn, that is. I spoke to lots to other people, just not to her. She seemed puzzled, though I couldn't imagine why. Did she seriously think that I would *want* to speak to her, after what she'd done?

At break I deliberately moved away when she came anywhere near. I couldn't have made it more obvious that I wanted nothing to do with her, but at lunchtime she still came and sat next to me, same as usual. *Some people*, I thought, *just couldn't take a hint.*

"Is everything all right?" she said.

For a moment I was tempted to ask someone further down the table to change seats with me, but I couldn't quite bring myself to do so. People would wonder what was wrong, and I didn't see that it was any of their business.

"Maddy?" Caitlyn was looking at me with a worried frown. "Are you OK?"

I said, "What do you think?"

How was I supposed to be OK when my best friend had gone behind my back and got me into trouble? When I probably wasn't going to be in the Gala *at all*, not even as a stupid Clown, and might actually be in danger of being thrown out? And then she asked me if I was *OK?*

"Did you know," she said, "that Miki Karashima's got glandular fever?"

I grunted.

"Her name's still on the cast list, but apparently she's going to be off for the rest of the term, so maybe you'll get to dance the Spanish Doll after all!"

I didn't say anything to that, just speared a bit of lettuce off my plate.

"They'll have to decide soon," said Caitlyn.

I speared another bit of lettuce. Horrible boring stuff!

"If you're talking about Miss Hickman," I said, "she's already decided."

"So are you going to get the part?"

I said, "Of course I'm not going to get the part!" Did she honestly believe that Miss Hickman would give it to me? *Now?*

"But… why not?"

Why did she think? Silently I held up my wrist.

"So it's only a bruise! Didn't you tell her? It's not going to stop you dancing!"

I said, "No, she is."

"She's going to stop you dancing?"

Caitlyn's eyes were full of concern. *Pretend* concern.

"It seems you were right," I said. "I'm not committed enough."

I obviously said it louder than I intended. A startled silence fell over the table. Eyes swivelled in my direction.

"According to Miss Hickman," I said.

"She actually said that?" Roz's voice had gone all shrill with indignation. "She said you weren't committed enough? Just because you hurt your wrist?"

"It was hardly your fault," said Alex. "Some great clumsy idiot goes crashing into you, how are you to blame?"

"You did tell her how it happened?"

Pointedly, not looking at Caitlyn, I said, "I didn't have to. She already knew. So how—"

"Omigod!" Amber's voice suddenly came screeching

up from the far end of the table. She clapped a hand to her mouth and stared, wide-eyed and dramatic, over the top of it. "Omigod, I'm so sorry! What have I done?"

The eyes all switched from me to Amber. It was Caitlyn, in a small, accusing voice, who said, "What *have* you done?"

"I told Miss Eldon!"

"Told her what?" I said.

"About the… you know! The ice skating?"

I flicked a glance at Caitlyn. I could see she was every bit as taken aback as I was.

"I didn't mean to," said Amber. "Honestly! It just slipped out."

"How's it supposed to have done that?" said Caitlyn. "'*Just slipped out?*'"

"It just did!" Amber rolled her eyes, wildly. "She was asking me how my toe was, cos you know I stubbed it and it went all blue? So we got talking about injuries and I said how Maddy's wrist looked really bad, but at least it wasn't broken, which it could well have been, cos I mean, like, accidents on the ice can be quite dangerous, especially for a dancer, which was why Caitlyn had tried to stop... Oops!" She clamped a hand back to her mouth.

"You brought *me* into it?" said Caitlyn.

"I'm sorry, I'm so sorry! Me and my big mouth! It's just that we were talking and I said how you'd tried to stop her and—"

"Who told you that?" I said.

"My friend Sonya? She felt really bad! She said she thought afterwards she shouldn't have let you do it, but you really seemed to want to and if it hadn't been for that stupid boy you'd have been OK. She said you were really good! She was really impressed."

"What did Miss Eldon say? When you told her," said Caitlyn. "Was she cross?"

"She didn't sound it. Not specially."

"So what did she say?"

"She just said... '*So Maddy went ice skating and had*

an accident.' Or something like that. I can't remember exactly."

"And then she went and told Miss Hickman."

"Well… yes. I suppose."

"Omigod, you are such an *idiot!*" cried Alex.

I thought at first she meant me, but it seemed she was talking to Amber.

Amber hung her head. "I truly didn't mean to," she said.

"I don't see why you should have to apologise," said Tiffany. "If she hadn't gone skating in the first place, it wouldn't have happened."

"Oh, shut up," said Roz. "Stop being so self-righteous!"

They were all on my side, except for Tiffany. Even Amber seemed genuinely sorry for what she'd done.

"D'you think it really did just slip out?" said Caitlyn, as we left the refectory together.

I thought about it. I didn't much care for Amber, but I didn't want to falsely accuse her. I know from experience how easy it is to just open your mouth and say things that you later wish you hadn't.

"I can't believe she'd do it on purpose," I said. "I mean… why would she?"

Caitlyn didn't say anything to that. She didn't have to. The look she gave me said it all: *Why did you think that I had done it?* She obviously didn't want to ask the question any more than I wanted to answer it. I think we both felt it would be better not to talk about it. We were back to being friends again; that was what mattered.

"Was Miss Hickman really mad at you?" said Caitlyn.

"Absolutely furious! She says I'll be lucky to be in the Gala at all."

"But that's so not fair! All you did was just go ice skating."

"It wasn't only the ice skating." I drew a breath, warding off tears. This was Caitlyn, not Sean. I couldn't cry all over Caitlyn! "Carey wanted me for the Spanish Doll right from the start, but Miss Hickman wouldn't let her have me cos she said –" I drew another breath – "she said my attitude wasn't right. She said it was the reason they didn't accept me straight away like they did you. She said I was a borderline case and they nearly didn't offer me a place at all. It's like what you said." I pressed my fingers under my eyes, keeping the tears held in. "I've had it too easy!"

"I shouldn't have said that," said Caitlyn. "You were right: I was just jealous."

I shook my head, vehemently. "I never believed that for one moment! It was a horrid thing to accuse you of."

"I was a bit envious, though," said Caitlyn.

"Well!" I gave a little laugh. *Tried* to give a little laugh. "You don't have to be envious now. You're more likely to be the one who ends up in the Company, not me. I'll be lucky if I even get to come back next term!"

⋆ Chapter Twelve

Next morning, as I was on my way out, Mum asked me the question I'd been dreading: "Have you heard yet what you'll be doing for the Gala?"

"Um… no," I said. "Not yet."

Mum frowned. "They're leaving it rather late, aren't they?"

"It's only short little bits and pieces," I said. "Nothing longer than about ten minutes. It doesn't take much to learn."

"I would remind you," said Mum, "that even something which only lasts ten minutes can be a little gem. In fact the shorter it is, the more it's up to you to make sure that every step counts — not just for your own satisfaction, but for your choreographer, as well. It's a showpiece for both of you. You need to take it seriously! Don't just dismiss it as bits and pieces."

I met up with Caitlyn on the way in to school. "Mum's been lecturing me," I said.

"About what?" said Caitlyn.

I pulled a face. "The Gala. She doesn't think I'm taking it seriously. I don't know what she's going to say when she discovers I'm not even in it."

"Oh, but, Maddy, you will be! You must be! I can't believe even Miss Hickman would be mean enough to stop you dancing."

"She could." I said it glumly. "It's what she was threatening… She mightn't even let Carey have me as one of her stupid Clowns."

"Your name was still up there yesterday," said Caitlyn.

"Yes, I know, but so was Miki's," I said. "And she's *definitely* not going to be able to dance."

"Let's go and look!" Caitlyn darted ahead of me,

down the stairs towards the bulletin boards. "See if anything's changed."

Nothing had: Miki's name was still there as the Spanish Doll and I was still there as one of the Clowns.

"That's got to be a good sign," said Caitlyn. "It must mean she's still considering. Don't you think?"

"Maybe," I said. I didn't hold out much hope. Miss Hickman had made it very clear: she didn't believe I deserved a part in the Gala. Why would she change her mind?

We passed Carey on our way back up the stairs. She didn't say anything, just pursed her lips and rather coolly shook her head. I wondered if she was also going to look at the bulletin boards – or whether, maybe, she had heard from Miss Hickman and it was not good news.

At lunchtime, for some reason, Caitlyn didn't appear so I sat next to Alex, who was still full of indignation on my behalf.

"It's that beastly, Amber," she said, though she didn't actually say the word *beastly*, she said another word that we're not supposed to use. I had used it once when I got a bit overheated about something. Actually I'd used *two* words: one beginning with *B* and one with *H*. Both equally bad. Apparently. One of the teachers had taken me aside and said, "We don't employ that sort of language, Maddy, no matter how strongly we feel."

It was not unusual for me to be told off; I just seem to be the sort of person who naturally does everything wrong. Alex, on the other hand, almost never does, so I knew how cross she had to be with Amber and her great clacking tongue.

"It's so unfair," she said. "You work just as hard as the rest of us! How can they accuse you of not being committed, just because of this one thing?"

I said, "It's not just this one thing. They've always thought I'm not committed, right from the beginning."

"But why?"

"It's because of who you are," said Chloe. "Cos of your mum and dad, and everything. They probably reckon you need keeping down in case you get too grand and start thinking you're someone special."

I was indignant. "I've never in my life thought I'm anyone special!"

"No, but you know what they're like. It's the way their minds work. If they don't stamp on you now and again, they're scared you'll get above yourself."

"Now and again would be one thing," said Alex. "But *not letting her dance in the Gala*? That's just spiteful!"

"Oh, what does it matter?" I suddenly felt that all the fight had gone out of me. Miss Hickman obviously thought I was worthless; even Mum had had her doubts. "Maybe they're right, maybe I'm *not* committed enough. I'll probably end up doing topless dancing in some sleazy nightclub."

Someone giggled. Alex stared at me, reproachfully.

"That would be a total *waste*."

"But fun," said Chloe.

"It wouldn't be fun!" Alex rounded on her, angrily.

"It'd be utterly stupid. She only said it cos she's trying to be brave and pretend she doesn't care."

I said, "Maybe I really *don't* care."

Just for a moment, I almost didn't. What more did they want from me? I'd never resented criticism; I'd never relied on family connections; I hadn't even let Sean go and talk to Madam. I'd always done the very best I could. And still it wasn't enough!

Darkly Roz said, "There's always people they have it in for. Look at Kate Kelly! She said in her autobiography how she thought she was going to be thrown out cos for some reason they took against her, and then she ended up one of the stars of the Company! It just goes to show."

"Yes. Well." They were all being so supportive! I blinked, rapidly, and quickly changed the subject. "Does anyone happen to know where Caitlyn is? Has anyone seen her?"

It seemed that nobody had. I wondered where she could have gone. She'd been there all morning and then just disappeared, without a word to anyone. She arrived in the refectory just as we were leaving.

"Where have you been?" I said. "You haven't had any lunch!"

"I know, I'm going to go and grab a sandwich. I'm sorry, I should have told you. I was called for an extra rehearsal."

I said, "Oh. How's it going?"

I had to force myself to ask. I really didn't care any more. About anything.

Caitlyn said brightly that things were going well. "Joyce is really easy to work with."

"Joyce Wang?" said Mei. "Didn't I see her having lunch?"

"Oh! Yes, well, you might have done. She wasn't actually *at* the rehearsal. It was just me. I wanted to run through things by myself and make sure I'd got it right. You know?"

Caitlyn's face had turned a giveaway pink. She was making it up! She hadn't been at an extra rehearsal at all. I looked at her, suspiciously. What was going on? Was she trying to keep something from me? Some sort of good news that she didn't want me to know about... Surely *she* couldn't have been chosen to appear in *Nutcracker*? I could see it would be difficult, breaking it to me. She probably thought I would be hurt. Even jealous, which was what I'd accused her of. But I wouldn't be! I really wouldn't! I wouldn't let myself. It would be very hard to bear, though.

At the end of the afternoon someone gave me a message from Miss Preedy: Miss Hickman wanted to see me before I went home. I didn't know what to think. She had obviously come to some sort of decision... but what?

I told Caitlyn to go on without me. "There's no point hanging around."

"I can wait for you," she said.

"No," I said, "don't! If it's bad news, I'll just want to run away and hide."

"But it might not be bad news! I'll wait," said Caitlyn,

"and if you don't want to talk you can just pull a face, like this –" she turned down the corners of her mouth – "and I'll walk away. On the other hand, if you give a big *smile* – like this…"

I didn't even want to think about it. It was a lovely fantasy, but I couldn't afford to indulge in it. Better to face up to reality and prepare for the worst.

Heart hammering, I delivered myself to Miss Preedy.

"Ah," she said, "you got my message. Miss Hickman's expecting you; you can go straight in."

"Madeleine." Miss Hickman studied me across the acres of her desk. "No need to sit down; this won't take long."

I swallowed. My heart was banging and thudding, hurling itself about inside my ribcage. I tried to take a steadying breath, but all I could manage were a few quick gulps of air.

"Much against my better judgement," said Miss Hickman, "I have allowed myself to be swayed by some very persuasive pleading on your behalf."

Sean.

"Oh," I cried, "I told him not to!"

Miss Hickman raised an eyebrow. "I'm sorry?"

"Sean! I told him not to! I didn't want you thinking I was asking for special treatment just cos of him being in the Company, and cos of Mum and Dad, and..." My voice trailed off, into a self-pitying whimper. "I did tell him!"

"I'm glad to hear that," said Miss Hickman. "I would certainly not have reacted well. As it happens, however, it was not Sean; it was Caitlyn."

Caitlyn? She was the one who had spoken up for me?

"She is a very loyal friend," said Miss Hickman. "She was telling me how you had helped her, and about the sacrifice you had made, letting her take your place in your school's end-of-term show so that your mother could see what she was capable of. If it hadn't been for you, I gather she would not be here with us today."

I squirmed, uncomfortably. I didn't know what to say.

"I was, of course, partly aware," said Miss Hickman.

"I knew she'd had a late start and a bit of a struggle. I just didn't realise how great a part you had played. So!" Miss Hickman sat back on her chair. "The decision I have reached is this: you will be allowed to participate in the Gala and you will be allowed to dance the part for which Carey originally wanted you. It is, as I say, against my better judgement – I still have grave misgivings, so I would caution you, Maddy, to take to heart the warning you have been given and prove yourself worthy of this second chance. Do I make myself clear?"

I swallowed again. I said, "Yes, Miss Hickman."

"Very well. I have informed Carey and she is looking forward to working with you. Please be sure not to let her down."

"I won't," I said. "Honestly!"

"Right. Well, off you go, then – and whatever you do, no more ice skating, please."

I said, "No, Miss Hickman."

As I left the Office, trying not to make my step too springy or my smile too broad, Miss Preedy said, "All right?" And she gave a little nod of encouragement, almost like she was happy for me.

Caitlyn was waiting at the exit as promised. She searched my face, anxiously. I sent her a big beam.

"It's all right! It's OK!"

"Oh, Maddy, I'm so glad!" Caitlyn flung her arms round me. "That is such a relief! I couldn't bear the thought of you not being in the Gala! I don't suppose she's letting you have the part you wanted?"

"She is! She actually says I can dance the Spanish Doll!"

A look of satisfaction appeared on Caitlyn's face. "I knew she would!"

"I honestly don't think she was going to," I said. "It's only thanks to you."

"*Me?* I didn't do anything!"

"You spoke to her," I said. "She told me."

"Oh! She didn't have to do that."

"She said you'd pleaded with her. I thought at first it was Sean! He wanted to have a word with Madam for me, but I wouldn't let him. I don't know how you found the courage. Even Sean's terrified of Miss Hickman!"

Not quite true, but I did think it was incredibly loyal of Caitlyn.

She blushed. "I had to at least try," she said. "I couldn't let her treat you that way after all you'd done for me." She suddenly looked uncertain. "I hope you didn't mind?"

I said, "Mind?" *How could she think I would mind?*

"If you didn't want Sean to do it."

"Only because he's family," I said. "It's different if it's a friend."

"That's what I thought." Caitlyn nodded, happily. "It's what friends are for. You didn't *really* think I was the one that gave you away, did you?"

It was my turn to blush.

"Don't worry," said Caitlyn. "Even I couldn't think how she'd found out... I just knew it wasn't me!"

The first thing I did on arriving home was tell Mum.

"The cast lists have gone up for the Gala. I'm dancing

a Spanish Doll! *The* Spanish Doll. There's only one," I assured her.

"Excellent," said Mum. "Sounds like fun. What about Caitlyn? What's she doing?"

"Oh, some winter thing… the Spirit of Winter. Actually," I said, "it's a solo."

"Good for her," said Mum. "Good for both of you! I'm glad to know you're doing well."

The next thing I did, after telling Mum, was ring Sean.

"… and she said I can dance the original part I was wanted for and I thought it was cos you'd gone and talked to Madam like you said, but it wasn't, it was Caitlyn, I couldn't believe it, I—"

"Hang about, hang about," said Sean. "*I* can't believe you thought it was me! You expressly told me not to. You really thought I'd go against your wishes?"

"I just couldn't imagine who else it would be!"

"Like you just couldn't imagine who else could have told on you? I'm assuming you got that one wrong, as well, and that it wasn't Caitlyn at all."

I said, "No, it was some stupid girl in my year who's friends with the girl I went skating with. It just *seemed* like it had to be Caitlyn cos there wasn't anybody else that knew. I mean, I didn't *think* there was anybody else that knew, and neither did she, as a matter of fact, but then we'd sort of had words so…"

"So I take it you've kissed and made up?"

"No, cos we didn't quarrel," I said. "Not like you and Danny. We just said things."

"Oh! So that makes it all right, does it? You don't mind laying down the law to others!"

"I wasn't laying down the law, I was trying to help! And I am extremely grateful to you," I said, "for letting me cry all over you the other day."

"No problem! I reckon I owed you one. Interfering busybody though you are, it must have taken some courage to come barging your way in and have a go at me when I was all… what was it you called me? All mean and miserable?"

"You were," I said. "You were mean as could be!"

"Well, it was very brave of you," said Sean. "Just as it was very brave of Caitlyn to beard the Hickman in her den. I hope you've thanked her?"

"Not properly," I said. "But I've just had the most brilliant idea! Something that would be beyond her wildest dreams."

"What's that?"

"If you and Danny could come to the end-of-term Gala? She would so love it if you were there to see her dance! It could be my way of saying thank you."

Sean said, "*Your* way?" He sounded faintly amused for some reason.

"It's not much to ask," I said.

"No, and I'd be quite happy to come. There's only one small problem: it's strictly just for staff and students."

"I'm sure if you had a word with Madam—"

"Oh! So now she *wants* me to pull favours!"

"For Caitlyn," I begged. "Not for me. *Please*, Sean! She'd be over the moon."

"Well, I suppose if you put it that way… OK, OK,

I'll see what I can do. You just go and kiss and make up!"

I was so happy being the Spanish Doll! I loved it so much. I felt sorry for poor Miki with her glandular fever, but I couldn't help being glad that it was me dancing the part and not her, especially as everyone kept saying how right I was for it. Even Carey! She told me that it was me who'd originally inspired her. She said she'd been searching for a suitable subject for her Gala piece when she'd happened to glance through the glass panels of the door to Studio Three one day when we were having class with Mr Alessandro.

"You were doing one of the dances from *Three-Cornered Hat,* and you were the one I found myself watching. I knew immediately that I wanted to use you. I wasn't quite sure how; I just knew that it had to be something Spanish. So then I thought of *Ballet of the Dolls*, and that's how it all came about. You," said Carey, "were my muse!"

I couldn't wait to get home that afternoon to tell Mum and Dad.

"You'll never guess," I said. "I'm a muse!"

They both looked a bit puzzled.

"Amused by what?" said Mum.

"No, a *muse*," I said. "I'm someone's muse! Like when Dad gets inspired by people and writes ballets for them? I've had a ballet written for me! Well, not the *whole* ballet, but the part I'm dancing."

"The Spanish Doll?" said Mum.

"Yes! Carey says she saw me when we were learning one of the dances from *Three-Cornered Hat* and knew immediately that she had to use me!"

"Excellent," said Mum. "A great start to your career."

"It's how it happens," agreed Dad. "Catch the eye of a budding choreographer and you're all set. So long as you get on together…"

"We do!" I said.

"Well, that's what's needed," said Dad. "Having faith in each other."

I hadn't had much faith in poor Carey originally, when I thought I was going to be stuck as a stupid Clown. I felt guilty about it now, especially as I couldn't have got it more wrong about the Clowns. They weren't stupid at all. It was only when we had the final rehearsal and I got to see the full ballet for the first time that I realised. They were funny and clever and inventive. Their costumes were inventive, too. Part of the challenge of the end-of-term Gala was having to provide for ourselves. We couldn't just trot along to Wardrobe and beg for something to wear, and we weren't allowed to hire anything, or to spend more than five pounds, tops. The idea was that we should use our ingenuity and imagination.

It had been easy enough for me. I simply wore a flouncy skirt that Jen had given me – and that I had altered *all by myself* – with a long-sleeved leotard, my character shoes and a red fringed shawl that Mum had let me have. It was easy for Caitlyn, too. As the Spirit of Winter she had chosen all white: white leotard, white tights, white shoes, with white glitter in her hair. The only spot of colour was a spray of red berries.

It was a bit more difficult for some of the others.

The Clowns, for example. They all had full clown make-up, with pointy hats made of cardboard and held on with elastic, and were wearing the grey sweatshirts and jogging pants that were part of our winter uniform, with pom-poms sewn on to the front of the sweatshirts. To get the clown effect they had obviously borrowed the pants from older students as they were all baggy and had to be kept up with braces. Instead of big clown boots they had on ordinary ballet shoes, which just added to the comic effect. We were all genuinely impressed, though I was still glad I wasn't one of them!

The Gala was always held on the last Saturday of term, in the afternoon. I rang Sean the night before just to check that he and Danny were going to be there.

"So that we can be your treat?" said Sean. He still seemed to find it amusing, though I couldn't think why. He and Danny *were* my treat: my treat for Caitlyn. It was my way of thanking her for what she had done. What was so funny about that?

"Oh, we'll be there," said Sean, "never fear. I've

promised Madam we'll hide ourselves away in the gallery and be quiet as mice."

I said, "Yes, cos if people saw you they'd get all silly and screechy."

"You don't think maybe we should come in disguise?"

I frowned. I am never quite sure with Sean when he is being serious and when he is teasing.

"I don't think I'd better tell Caitlyn," I said. "Not till afterwards."

"You mean in case *she* gets all silly and shrieky?"

"No, in case she goes into meltdown." I giggled. "She's the Spirit of Winter so she needs to stay frozen!"

"OK, well, let's all meet up in the refectory after the show. Meanwhile, break a leg!"

There were a lot of pre-performance nerves in our dressing room as we got ready the next day. The performances might not be open to the public, but the whole school was going to be out there, watching and passing judgement – and, of course, Madam and the rest of the staff, all beady-eyed and on the lookout for faults.

"It's like having an audition all over again," moaned Alex.

"It is an audition," said Amber. "Good as."

I thought, *Yes, and for me especially.* I knew Miss Hickman still had doubts. I could actually be thrown out! People had been known to disappear at the end of their first term. Not very often, it was true; but it had happened.

"Does anybody know," said Roz, "if there's going to be a DVD?"

"I should hope so!" said Tiffany. "All this for just a few minutes of honour and glory and nothing to show for it?"

"It's OK, they always film it," I said. "They do it for the choreographers more than us."

"But we can get copies?"

"If we want them," I said.

Tiffany tossed her head. "I want one!"

"Mum does, too," I said. "She's still got the ones from when Sean and Jen were in their first year."

"Oh, I wish I could see them!" cried Caitlyn, and then immediately blushed furiously and clapped a hand to her mouth.

"It's all right," said Roz, kindly. "We all know how you feel about a certain person."

"No!" Caitlyn shook her head, spraying silver glitter all over the place. "I meant Jen! I wish I could see Jen!"

"Don't worry, you can see them both," I said.

I felt like adding, "You can even see one of them here today," but I resisted the temptation. The atmosphere in the dressing room was already tense; knowing who was up in the gallery would only make it worse. There are people like me, and like Tiffany – bigheaded, some would say – who never really suffer from stage fright. Others, such as Caitlyn, can be almost crippled by it. It might throw her completely if she knew that Sean was up in the gallery.

Winter Dreams was the opening piece. It only lasted

five minutes, but as Mum said later, when we watched the DVD together, "Every one of those minutes counted." Jen's comment was, "Exquisite!" At the time, waiting in the wings till it was my turn to go on, I was a bit too fraught to take in all the details, but there was a collective intake of breath, from me and some of the others, as Caitlyn performed her final reverence.

"Who can hope to beat that?" whispered Alex.

"Well, it's her sort of part," said Tiffany.

Tiffany was right, it *was* Caitlyn's sort of part: poised, and elegant, and as Dad said, as we watched the DVD, an almost other-worldly beauty. As different as could be from the knockabout humour of the Clowns, or the swirling excitement of the Spanish Doll. But saying it was "*her sort of part*", in that slightly sneering way that Tiffany had, didn't make it any less an amazing performance. It was hard to believe that only two years ago she had never so much as had a single ballet lesson. She had come so far since that day in the gym, when I had discovered her desperately trying to teach herself how to do pirouettes. I remembered teaching her, and how quickly she had learnt. In spite of her technique still not being as strong as mine, I had this feeling that she was catching up fast. Which was good! What teacher wouldn't want her pupil to do well? We would always be very different kinds of dancer. The Spanish Doll was my sort of part, just as the Spirit of Winter was Caitlyn's. We weren't really in competition.

As I stood in the wings, waiting to make my entrance, Nico came up and squeezed my arm.

"Go for it, girl!"

I smiled at him, gratefully. He knew how much depended on my performance. For maybe the first time in my life, I felt that I was being put to the test. I couldn't afford to fail! It would be letting everyone down. Not only Mum and Dad, but Sean, who had stood up for me; Caitlyn, who had been so loyal; even Miss Hickman, who had given me a second chance. I owed it to all of them to do my very best.

The moment came. I ran on stage and took up my position: back arched, arms raised. I was the Spanish Doll. *Olé!*

I danced as I had never danced before. Stamping, spinning, twisting. Just five short minutes and every one of them filled with passion. I had never felt so exhilarated! I felt like I could go on for ever.

"Maddy, that was so exciting!" said Caitlyn, after we had all taken our bows at the end.

"Spanish Dancing *is* exciting," I said. "And you know what?"

"What?"

I was almost on the point of saying, "There's something else that's exciting!" but stopped myself just in time. I didn't want to spoil the surprise! "Let's get changed and go up to the refectory."

Caitlyn looked puzzled. "I thought we were going straight home. Why do we want to go to the refectory?"

I said, "Cos we do. Don't argue!"

Meekly she followed me. My plan was almost ruined at the last moment by Tiffany galloping after us.

"Did I hear you guys saying you were going to get something to eat? I wouldn't mind something to eat! I'm starving. Can I tag along?"

"Actually," I said, "we're meeting someone."

"Oh. Well. OK!" She tossed her head, like, *I can tell when I'm not wanted.* "I'll see if Amber wants to come."

"So who are we going to meet?" whispered Caitlyn, as we left the dressing room.

"Just wait," I said, "and you'll see."

Her face, when we reached the refectory and found Sean and Danny sitting there, was full of wonderment.

"They were up in the gallery," I said. "They came specially to watch your performance!"

"We did," said Sean. "Congratulations… the pair of you! Mum's going to be like a cat that's got the cream when she sees what you both did. Great stuff! It really was most impressive."

By now, needless to say, Caitlyn had turned a bright blushing pink. Danny, taking pity on her, said, "Let's go and get you something to eat. You coming, Maddy? Oh, and by the way, I managed to get a few photographs of you both, for the book. Madam said it'd be OK. I just need to get permission to use them. Well, I know I can use Caitlyn's, but, Maddy, you'll need to check with your mum and dad. Sean doesn't seem to think there'll be any problem. I hope not, cos it would be good to have you in there."

I was so thrilled at the thought of being in Danny's book that my face actually started to turn as pink as Caitlyn's. I could feel it happening! It wasn't embarrassment: just happiness. I hadn't properly realised until now how hurt I'd been when I'd heard that Caitlyn was going to be in the book and not me.

"So," said Sean, as we made our way back to the table, "did you kiss and make up?"

Caitlyn looked at me, questioningly.

"He thinks we quarrelled," I said.

"We wouldn't ever do that," protested Caitlyn.

"That's what I told him! We just had words."

"You harboured ill feelings," said Sean.

"Oh, that's right, she did," agreed Caitlyn. "She thought I'd told Miss Hickman about her! Which was mean," she added, "cos I never would."

"It was only because we'd said things," I pleaded. "Cos I'd said you were jealous, which I *knew* wasn't true, and you got mad at me, and so I thought that's why you might have done it."

"But you were wrong," said Sean. "The least you can do is kiss and say sorry."

"Oh, all right!" I pecked furiously at Caitlyn's cheek. "Sorry, sorry, sorry!"

"Call that a kiss?" jeered Sean.

"It's better than you did," I said. "You were *pathetic*."

"Yeah? I can set that right if you want. Do you want me to?"

I glanced a bit nervously over my shoulder. "Miss Hickman's just come in," I said. "She can see us!"

"Think that would bother me?"

Caitlyn giggled. Danny tapped Sean on the back of the hand. "Stop showing off."

"Oh, very well," said Sean. "I'll make do with Caitlyn, instead." He leaned across and gave her a chaste kiss on the forehead. "Thank you for speaking up for my *very* annoying little sister. I don't know where she'd be without you."

Caitlyn, predictably, turned pink to the very tips of her ears. "I don't know where I'd be without her."

"There," said Sean. He beamed at us across the table. "Isn't that nice?"

I made a gurgling sound.

"*Now* what's the matter?"

"It's Miss Hickman," I whispered. "She's coming over!"

"All right, you don't have to panic. Just give her a big smile and—"

"Madeleine." Miss Hickman had stopped directly in front of me. I felt my heart sink. She looked as grim as ever. "And Caitlyn! Very well done, you two girls. Lovely performances from both of you."

Phew! Someone – I bet it was Sean – trod on my foot under the table.

"You obviously took my words to heart," said Miss Hickman, nodding almost pleasantly at me. "Thank you for not letting me down." And then she stretched her lips in a sort of smile and said, "Enjoy the holidays! I shall look forward to seeing you both next term."

Caitlyn and I sat watching, in awed silence, as Miss Hickman made her way to the door.

"Well, there you go," said Sean. "I told you there was no need to panic."

"Oh," I said, "you're always right!"

"I like to think so."

"Always so bigheaded," I grumbled.

"And one of us always so ungrateful," said Sean.

Danny and Caitlyn exchanged glances.

Danny shook his head. "This is what passes for

brother-and-sisterly love? Shall we go and see if there's anything else we want to eat and just leave them to it? They might be a bit more civilised by the time we get back."

We wouldn't be, cos it was just our way. Sean knew I wasn't really ungrateful. I owed so much, both to him and to Caitlyn. Suddenly I was just dying to get home and tell Mum what Miss Hickman had said! *"Very well done, very lovely performances…"*

You couldn't get much higher praise than that!

If you loved STAR QUALITY, don't forget to read about Maddy and Caitlyn in BORN TO DANCE

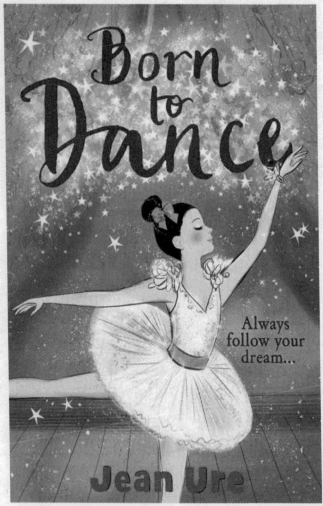

Maddy and Caitlyn will return with their next dance adventure in 2018

More from Jean Ure...

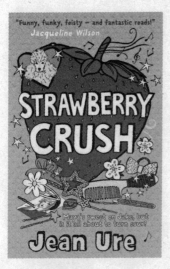

"Funny, funky, feisty – and fantastic reads!"
Jacqueline Wilson

SECRET MEETING

Jean Ure

"Funny, funky, feisty – and fantastic reads!"
Jacqueline Wilson

LEMONADE SKY

Jean Ure

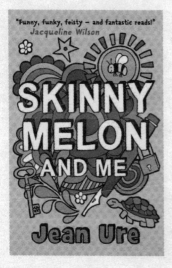

"Funny, funky, feisty – and fantastic reads!"
Jacqueline Wilson

SKINNY MELON AND ME

Jean Ure

"Funny, funky, feisty – and fantastic reads!"
Jacqueline Wilson

PUMPKIN PIE

Jean Ure

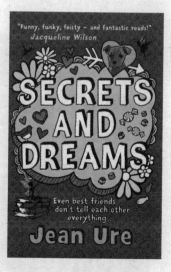

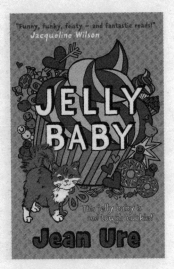

"Funny, funky, feisty – and fantastic reads!"
Jacqueline Wilson

JELLY BABY

The jelly baby is
one tough cookie!

Jean Ure

"Funny, funky, feisty – and fantastic reads!"
Jacqueline Wilson

LOVE AND KISSES

Jean Ure

"Funny, funky, feisty – and fantastic reads!"
Jacqueline Wilson

THE KISSING GAME

Who's ready
to play?

Jean Ure

And for fans of FRANKIE FOSTER...